Getting Wound Up

Sapphire Falls and Love Between the Bases Novel

Jennifer Bernard and Erin Nicholas

ISBN: 978-0-9965902-7-3

Editor: Kelli Collins
Cover artist: Valerie Tibbs
Digital formatting: Author E.M.S.
Print formatting: Kim Brooks

DEDICATION

To Friends

Getting Wound Up

CHAPTER ONE

"Bottom of the ninth, two out, here comes the fastball…"

Eli Anderson snagged the spinning object inches from his face.

"And it's in for a strike! Nice play, boss!" called the stock boy from the plumbing aisle.

Eli looked down at the roll of plumber's tape in his hand. *Riiiiight.* He wasn't on the mound at Royals Stadium, the University of Nebraska campus, the Sapphire Falls community park or even his backyard. He was behind the counter at Anderson's Hardware. Where he spent about eighty percent of his waking hours.

He flipped the tape back to Jimmy. It hit the stock boy square in the chest, dropping into his grasp with a sweet little dip.

Jimmy whistled. "That knuckleball ought to be knocking 'em dead in Royals Stadium."

"Yeah right. Come on, we have to get that box unpacked by the time Dad gets here. You don't want the Glare of Doom, do you?"

"Rather get a fastball to the head," Jimmy groaned.

"I'll distract him with my sloppy purchase orders." Eli winked at the kid. Truth was, his father, Chip Anderson, didn't do much at the store these days. The massive stroke he'd suffered six years ago had taken away much of his mobility and his independence. It had taken three years of hard work before he could even speak. Eli had left college after the stroke and had been running the store since then. Eli knew how tough it was for Chip to rely on him, so he made sure to find ways his dad could feel useful. Like correcting purchase orders. Eli could do the P.O.s in his sleep, but instead he'd let his father grump his way through them.

Right on time, his father's wheelchair whispered down the ramp that led from the back entrance. He shot a look at Jimmy, whose unpacking immediately became ten times more industrious, then wheeled to Eli's side. Eli pushed the pile of orders toward him and crossed his arms over his chest, letting him look them over at his leisure.

Eli used the time to mentally retrace the "pitch" he'd thrown to Jimmy. Imagine throwing that during the World Series. *Perfect pitch, right in the corner, but what the heck did Anderson just throw across the plate? Is that...plumper's tape? Another first for Sapphire Falls' finest, Eli Anderson, who is flat-out revolutionizing the game of baseball, one bizarro pitch at a time.*

Eli started at the jab of his father's elbow in his side. "Yeah, Dad?"

His father was scowling at the paperwork. "You left out a decimal point."

"Oops. Thanks for catching that." Eli fixed the error that he'd put there on purpose, then met his father's eyes.

Damn. Busted. Judging from the way he rolled his eyes, his father knew exactly what he'd just done.

"You don't fool me, Eli."

"Sorry, Dad," Eli muttered. The chime at the door rang, and he looked up eagerly, anxious for a rescue.

Rescue had never looked prettier than it did in the form of Caitlyn Murray. Jimmy must have thought so too, because he dropped a roll of tape on his toe, then hopped up and down with a grimace. Poor slob. Eli gave a moment of thanks that he'd grown up with Caitlyn, that she was the little sister of his good friend Bryan and therefore he was automatically immune to her. Being a red-blooded American male, he could appreciate every bit of her petite, bright-eyed, blond-haired form. But he, unlike Jimmy, could enjoy the sight of her without any pesky inappropriate thoughts.

"Hi Eli, Mr. Anderson," Caitlyn called as she waltzed

through the door. She wore a short denim skirt and a white blouse tied in a knot at her tiny waist. She always complained about the size of her butt, but try as he might, Eli couldn't find a single problem with it. "Hey Jimmy."

Jimmy, still hopping on one foot, toppled backwards and stumbled against the shelving that held the plastic elbow pipes.

Eli cringed. *Get a grip*, he mouthed to Jimmy, who turned bright scarlet. Way to represent the male gender.

As usual, Caitlyn didn't seem to notice the effect she had. Eli admired that about her. She was a down-to-earth sweetheart of a girl. A good friend...the best. She proved it once again by bending down to kiss Eli's father on the cheek.

"I have a special surprise for you," she told him. "Should be ready by tomorrow."

His eyes lit up. Caitlyn worked at Scott's Sweets, Sapphire Falls' candy shop, and her specialty was one-of-a-kind concoctions customized for the lucky recipient. Chip had a hard time chewing, so she made him special peanut butter truffles that melted in his mouth with no effort on his part.

Eli smiled at her, his heart lifting. When Caitlyn was around, the burden of Anderson's Hardware, his father, his family, and his entire responsibility-filled life felt lighter.

She was such a good friend.

"So what are you up to, Candy-girl?" He shuffled the purchase orders back into their file. "Did the temp gauge go out on the oven again?"

She kept a hand on Chip's shoulder. "Can't I come visit my favorite guys without a hardware emergency?"

"You're welcome anytime. Heck, you can move in."

Something flickered across her face, and he suddenly realized how that statement might be interpreted. He scrambled to cover up his error. "Truffles twenty-four seven Dad. How's that sound?"

Chip was enjoying his embarrassment. "Pretty girl and candy. Hard to say no to that."

Jimmy made some sort of whimpering sound from the plumbing aisle.

Caitlyn, who was looking adorably pink-cheeked, hurried past the moment. "Actually, I came to borrow you for a little while, Eli. I need your help. I found a car on Craigslist, and I need an expert opinion but Bryan's got a full day of PT and work and can't look at it with me."

"First of all, Sapphire Falls has Craigslist? Second, hell yes, you need a new car." Caitlyn drove a godawful mustard-colored Ford Focus that singlehandedly kept the Sapphire Falls mechanics in overpriced motor oil. "But I can't go until—" He broke off at a jab in his ribs from his father. "*Ow*. Dad, I can't. I've got orders to place and a couple of lumber deliveries. And it's two hours until closing. Can you wait until later, Caitlyn?"

She shrugged, her blond hair bouncing on her shoulders. "It's okay. I can handle it. I already talked to the guy on the phone and he seems totally cool. He says it's in excellent condition and drives great. I have a really good feeling about it." She turned to go, then added over her shoulder, "Oh, what does 'salvaged' mean? That's a good thing, right?"

Eli was out from behind the counter before he knew it. "Caitlyn, you can't do this alone. Just wait two hours, would you? The shop'll be closed, and—"

"I'll be fine," grumped his father. "You go on, you two."

"I'll help him out, boss," Jimmy piped up. "Between me and Mr. Anderson, we got this. Can't let any Craigslist creep take advantage of Caitlyn." Just saying her name, he turned bright red.

Caitlyn tossed her hair. "You guys are being ridiculous. I can absolutely handle this and I'm sorry I even asked. The invitation is revoked." She marched toward the door, with

Eli scrambling behind her.

"The hell it is. I'm coming with you, Cait. Cait!"

He rushed out the door after her, into the bright sunshine of July in Nebraska. Main Street was crowded with afternoon shoppers, and he nearly lost Caitlyn in the crowd. Good thing he'd recognize that hideous yellow Focus anywhere. He sprinted after her, sliding into the passenger seat at the same moment she hit the driver's side.

Oddly enough, she didn't seem as irritated as he'd expected. In fact, she wore a slightly smug expression as she started the car. Eli wondered if he'd been played, but then decided he didn't mind. Buying a new car was a very important job and he was the perfect guy to help her with it.

"I'm glad you came to me, Cait. Bryan would kill me if I let his little sis go car shopping alone."

Her smile vanished. She looked as though she was about to say something, but held herself back. "I really appreciate it," she said in a sweet voice. "You have no idea how much."

Something was strange in her tone, but he couldn't quite put his finger on it. "So where are we going? Where's this guy located? What kind of car is it?"

In answer, she turned up the volume on the speakers. The sound of Beyoncé filled the car, singing something about girls running the world.

Hell, Eli had no objection to that. A girl was certainly running his world at the moment. Two minutes ago he'd been facing more hours at the hardware store. Now, he was suddenly and unexpectedly free, as if school had let out early. He relaxed into the pleasure of the breeze whipping through the open window, the tunes rocking the car, Caitlyn's whistling in time to the music.

He glanced over at her and got momentarily lost in the way her lips pursed together to form the tune. Caitlyn had a very sexy mouth—why had he never noticed that before?

"So what ever happened to Dude-face?" he asked her.

"*Dude-face?*"

"You know, what's his name. With the beard."

"Ross. And FYI, beards are in right now. It's the whole lumbersexual thing."

"The what?"

"Lumbersexual. Have you been living under a rock? It's the new trend."

Eli laughed long and hard. The things Caitlyn found on Facebook cracked him up. "I sell lumber. Do I qualify?"

"No. You need a beard."

"I could grow a beard. Dare me?"

He, Caitlyn and Bryan had always dared each other to do silly crap like drink an entire bottle of Tabasco sauce. He'd almost always won those dares, because he'd been a reckless goofball until the age of nineteen. That's when his father had suffered the stroke and everything had gotten very serious, very quickly.

"Absolutely not. I kind of OD'd on the facial hair thing. Not that… I mean, it's totally different because you wouldn't be giving me whisker burn or making me sneeze when I kiss you or…" She snapped her mouth shut, her cheeks the color of carnations.

He laughed some more. Caitlyn was such a darling. It was really shocking no one had snatched her up yet, permanently. Of course, it would have to be someone worthy. Would *anyone* be worthy of Caitlyn? He wasn't at all sure about that. Hopefully she'd allow him to scope the guy out the way he was doing with this car they were about to see.

Speaking of which…looking around, he realized they were on the highway heading out of town. "Where the hell is this place?"

"Oh, it's just outside of Kingston."

He eyed her closely. Her lower lip was caught between her teeth, and her color was still high. A memory flashed into his mind of the time they'd "borrowed" Bazooka bubble gum from the convenience store, intending to come back with a dime. But Caitlyn hadn't even made it to the corner before she burst into tears and went running back with her half-opened loot.

"You're hiding something," he accused. "You're the worst liar in Sapphire Falls. What's going on?"

"Nothing! It's just a little farther…" Now she was looking just the way she had at the age of seven, tears gathering in her big hazel eyes.

"Caitlyn…"

"Okay, okay. There is no car." She whooshed out a breath, clearly relieved to not be lying anymore. "This is a…well, this is a kidnapping."

"*What?*"

She turned to look at him with an exasperated expression. "Have you forgotten what tomorrow is?"

It was a Saturday. In July. Nothing special. Not his birthday, not her birthday, not Bryan's birthday. He shrugged, at a complete loss.

"The tryout," she said gently. "The San Diego Friars' open tryout camp. The one the scout said you should go to after you got your fastball up to speed."

Eli's gut clenched as if someone had just rammed a fist into it. "Turn the car around."

"No."

"I'm not going to any fucking tryout, Cait."

She set her chin the way he and Bryan had seen a million times when they tried to boss her around. "Why not?"

"Because I'm a hardware store owner, not a ballplayer."

"That's crap. People are all sorts of things before they become ballplayers. How do you know if you don't give it a shot?"

"I can't, Caitlyn. You know why I can't." He couldn't believe she was making him spell it out.

"Because of your father? Well, guess what, he's

onboard with this plan. He knows exactly where you are right now. He even paid for the hotel room."

"*What?*"

That was impossible. His father needed him at home and at the store. Anderson's Hardware provided the entire family with its income, and Chip simply couldn't handle it anymore. Eli no longer had time for childish baseball fantasies. Okay, so he'd kept working out. Kept honing his pitches. Added leg strength to help his fastball. But that was just for fun, because he loved the fucking game. His mind had let go of the dream of a baseball career, even though maybe his heart hadn't.

Because right now it was beating so hard it might flop out of his chest.

"Yes, Eli. Your dad wants you to do this. So don't use him as an excuse."

"*Excuse?*" How could a stroke be considered an excuse? "I don't have any of my gear."

"It's in the trunk. Ty and Bryan packed it up."

Feeling a wave of dizziness, Eli gripped the handle on the passenger door. Ty and Bryan were in on this? Eli had always trailed after Bryan and Ty, the big star athletes, trying like hell to keep up. Ty was an Olympic triathlete, and Bryan was right up there with him—or had been before the accident that put him in a wheelchair part-time. Bryan had just moved back to Sapphire Falls from Denver about a year ago and had bought the Come Again, the only bar in town. He'd had the place remodeled so that he could manage it and bartend with his crutches, sitting on a stool or even in the wheelchair when necessary. Eli was still getting used to seeing one of his friends in a wheelchair. First his dad, and now Bryan. Sometimes life just wasn't fucking fair.

"Actually, Bryan was going to take you, but now he's got the bar and, of course, with the chair—" Caitlyn's voice caught slightly. "It's harder for him to just up and go now like he used to. And Ty's got his training and Hailey. So I offered. And if you don't go along with it, they're going to murder me. So I would really appreciate it if you would just…you know…cooperate."

"Like a good little kidnapping victim?"

"Exactly," she answered cheerfully. "In other words, we can do this the easy way or the hard way. The hard way, I get Bryan on the phone. Then we go back and tell your father that you chickened out."

Caitlyn was boxing him into a corner, but he just couldn't be mad about it. She was too adorable. Come to think of it, maybe that's why Ty and Bryan had sent her. "What's the easy way?"

"Here." She handed him her iPhone and pressed a play button. A video popped up. Bryan in his workout gear in the new gym—i.e, Ty's dining room outfitted with a new weight machine, recumbent bike and treadmill—Ty standing behind him.

Bryan addressed the camera first. "Dude, sorry for the ambush. But we thought it was the best way. Didn't want to give you a chance to pussy out. Sorry Caitlyn, if you're listening."

Caitlyn rolled her eyes.

Ty stepped in. "Eli, man, we never said this before because…well, we're guys. But out of the three of us, when it comes to athletics, you're the best. You have the most natural skill, and you're the best competitor. We took our shots. Now it's your turn."

Bryan leaned in to the camera. "You had to quit because of your dad, and that's cool. We both admire the hell out of you for that. But he's better now; at least he's better enough so you can make it work out. So we all got together and came up with this plan. Don't blame Caitlyn. She's just the messenger."

"She's more like a chauffeur than a messenger," Ty pointed out.

"Actually, she's more like a babysitter. She has our authorization to do whatever it takes to get you to that tryout. So watch your back, because you know how she is."

"Good luck, man."

"Knock 'em dead," added Bryan.

"Win or lose, might as well go down swinging, right?"

"It ain't over 'til it's over."

"'Til the fat lady sings."

Bryan scowled. "And he doesn't mean you, Caitlyn, so don't get all touchy about your butt."

Caitlyn reached over to snatch back the phone. "They go on like that for a while, but you get the gist." She wet her lips, looking a bit nervous. "Any questions?"

Eli was quiet for a long moment while his stomach churned like a freaking spin cycle.

Ever since he'd first picked up a baseball, it had felt like *his thing*. The right thing. The only thing. His father had taught him to play, even coached his Little League team. Like everyone else in Sapphire Falls, they'd rooted for the Kansas City Royals. He and his dad had even gone down to spring training a couple of times. He'd won a baseball scholarship to the University of Nebraska. He and his father had spent hours discussing his chances of playing for the Royals, and what he would do if—God forbid—the St. Louis Cardinals drafted him. Giving up the dream of pro baseball had been like cutting out a piece of his soul.

But he'd done it. And now he was supposed to just turn a one-eighty and pretend he still had a chance? Compete against guys who'd been training for this? Who had actually *planned* to be there tomorrow?

"Eli." Caitlyn's soft voice interrupted his panicky thoughts. "You can do this. And I'm not just saying that to make you relax. I've seen you working out. I've seen you throw. You. Can do this."

"I don't know, Caitlyn." With anyone else, he might have trouble expressing his self-doubt. But Caitlyn was different. "I don't want to go out there and make an ass out of myself."

"You won't. They're going to be blown away. Anyway, so what if you do? It's in Kansas City. No one will know except me. And if you're worried about making an ass out of yourself in front of *me*, you might want to rethink that booger wall next to your bed."

"I was *nine*. Are you ever going to let that go?"

"How can I? It's burned into my brain. It would take surgery to get it out. Which seriously might be an option. It was *so disgusting*." By now they were both laughing, and Eli realized all his anxiety had drained away. He shot her an appreciative look.

"You did that on purpose, didn't you?"

"What, re-traumatize myself to distract you? Yes." Her smug smile was completely adorable. "Did it work? Are you ready to play ball now?"

He sat up straighter, fingers flexing on his thighs, longing for a ball to handle. Suddenly, he couldn't wait to get on a mound, any mound, and show someone, anyone, what he could do. "Tell you what, Candy-girl. If I actually do this, if I actually pitch well enough to get a contract, we'll celebrate big."

"What do you mean?" She shot him a sidelong, nervous glance.

He winked back. "I'll buy you a car on Craigslist. This hunk of rust is a blight on the automotive world."

Sassy as ever, she stuck out her tongue as if she were six again. But damn…it had a whole different effect this time.

Little sister, he reminded himself. *Immune*. Besides, he had to focus on this amazing opportunity that had just sailed in from left field. Tryout camp. A chance to pitch before members of the Friars' scouting staff. And at nearly twenty-six years old, it was very likely his *last* chance.

CHAPTER TWO

Oh, if only Caitlyn could reach across the seats and deck Mr. Celebrate-Big-by-Buying-a-Car-on-Craigslist. But Eli wouldn't understand. And a bloody nose wouldn't help him at the tryout, and Ty and Bryan would *not* be happy with her. How would she explain it? "Eli keeps treating me like his little sister when I've been crushing on him hard for the past...oh...year and no one has even noticed? Especially him?"

No. Those words were locked in the vault. Forever. Or at least until Eli showed some awareness of the fact that she was a *female* of date-able age, single and generally considered attractive. Why was it so hard to drill that into his oblivious skull?

And how was she going to handle a night in a hotel room with him? Even now, on the road in her ugly mustard-mobile, her glance kept straying to his big hands as they rested on his thighs. If she had to pick one word to describe Eli, it would be "strong." Not just because of his powerful physique, which definitely qualified. Or because of his face, with its square jaw and clean, blue-eyed all-American look.

It was more because of the way he'd shouldered the entire burden of the family business without ever complaining. How he'd been there for his mother when she fell apart after Chip's stroke. How he'd gotten his sister Lindsay to school when his mother couldn't even get out of bed. Whatever progress Chip had made was at least partly thanks to Eli. The fact that Lindsay was one year from graduating high school at the top of her class—Eli's doing. The entire family would have collapsed without him.

Strong—that was Eli. Almost as strong as the crush that had been tormenting her for the past year. It was all Bryan's fault, really. If she hadn't followed him back to

Sapphire Falls after his accident, she would now be using her culinary arts degree at some five-star restaurant instead of at Scott's Sweets Shop. And she would still be in blissful ignorance of the magnificent, irresistible, sexy glory of Eli Anderson.

If Bryan had any idea how hard it was for her to be around Eli without throwing herself into his arms, he would never have sent her on this trip.

She tightened her grip on the steering wheel and glared at the highway. Hey, she was a big girl. She could handle herself around a hot guy, even one as devastating as Eli. She could do this.

"What'd that steering wheel ever do to you?" Eli's teasing drawl interrupted her. "I mean, aside from being attached to the biggest piece of junkyard scrap metal in Nebraska."

She seized on the chance to get back to familiar ground—teasing. "Are you going to mock my car the entire trip to Kansas?"

"Got any other ways to pass the time? I'm open."

"We could try conversing. That's a thing people do."

"Fine. Conversation it is. Ladies first."

She swallowed hard. Eli sure knew how to call a bluff. But this opportunity was too juicy to resist. "Why don't you have a girlfriend, Eli?"

He swung his head toward her, an astonished look on his face.

Really? Did he think she hadn't noticed his chronically single state? She'd been living in dread of him finally starting a real relationship.

"I have...women. I mean, one woman at a time."

"I know. For about a month. Then they're gone. And they're always about ten years older than you."

"Keeping track, are you?"

Yes. Lord, yes. Like "one step away from stalker" yes. But he didn't need to know that. "Lindsay's worried about you," she answered primly. "She asked me to find out what's wrong with you."

"There is nothing wrong with appreciating a slightly older woman who knows what she's doing."

Caitlyn seriously reconsidered her first idea of decking him right in the nose. But then Eli went on, in a more thoughtful tone.

"I guess...you know, I was only nineteen when my father had his stroke. The girls my age were still partying every night, same as I used to. I guess I just clicked more with women who'd been through some stuff. Seemed like I had more in common with them."

Caitlyn nodded, even more depressed now. She was two years younger than Eli. How could she ever catch up with those oh-so-experienced older women? No wonder he saw her only as some kid. It totally made sense.

But then...why didn't any of those relationships last?

Before she could ask him, he spoke again. "What about you? Not that I'm sad to see Dude-face go, but why aren't you replacing him with the next guy in line?"

"The next guy in *line*? What's that supposed to mean?"

"It means you could probably pick a random guy from the Sapphire Falls phone book and he'd want to date you. So who's next?"

Her face flamed. Was that what he thought? Seriously? "You're in the phone book," she blurted, only to feel her cheeks burn even hotter. *Smooth, Caitlyn. Really smooth.* "So that just proves you're wrong."

She felt his gaze and fought to keep her cool. *Change the subject, change the subject.* "So, do you think the Royals are going to win the World Series again this year? Would you mind playing for the Friars instead of the Royals? That might be kind of weird after an entire lifetime of rooting for the Royals. Do you think it would be hard to play against them?"

Thank the sweet Lord, he went for her change of topic.

"If the Friars sign me, I'll become an instant Friars fan. But I'd probably be playing for one of their farm teams. The Kilby Catfish, if I got really lucky. That's their Triple-A team. But I don't even want to talk about that. It's bad luck. One thing at a time. Let's just get to the tryout and see what happens."

He went back to drumming his fingers nervously on the car door, while she heaved a silent sigh of relief. She couldn't keep making little slips like that. Revealing her crush would be mortifying. Sapphire Falls was a small town, and everyone knew everyone else's business. It was a miracle no one had guessed already. But if Eli himself knew? And rejected her, or *pitied* her for her unrequited lust? Ouch!!! She'd still have to see him every other day because he ran the only hardware store in town, and her brother was his friend, and she knew his family and…ugh, it would be the *worst*. Everyone would feel awkward and sorry for her. She'd rather move to Borneo than go through that. And she couldn't move to Borneo because Bryan needed her.

For Bryan's sake, she needed to keep her stupid hopeless feelings to herself.

But…her crush whispered…what if he does get signed? What if he leaves town to play professional baseball? What if you *don't* have to see him every day?

Fine, she told herself firmly. *If Eli gets an actual contract that takes him away from Sapphire Falls, I'll reassess the situation.* "Celebrate big." *The way I want to celebrate.*

Eli spent the rest of the drive mentally rehearsing pitches and going over the information Caitlyn had downloaded from the Internet. Open tryout camps were basically the last resort for guys who hadn't been chosen in the draft, for whatever reason. Or people like him, whose lives had veered in different directions. There were a few stories of major leaguers who had been discovered at open tryouts, but not very many. Mostly, the machinery of Major League Baseball was pretty damn good at tracking down the players with potential. If he'd stayed in college, he might have been drafted. Who was he kidding? He *would* have been drafted. Pitchers were always in demand, and he'd been a rising star on one of the Big Ten's best teams.

But that was then, and this was now. At this point in his life, without consistent playing time against batters who could test him, without coaching from the experts, his chances were statistically very low.

But statistics didn't tell the whole story, he reminded himself. Even baseball fanatics who knew all the stats recognized that.

The tryout was scheduled to start at nine the next morning. They arrived at the hotel, an unassuming lodge near the college campus, around seven in the evening. Stretching the kinks out of his shoulders, Eli hauled Caitlyn's bag, along with the one Bryan had packed for him, into Room 112 while Caitlyn finished checking them in. As soon as he spotted the two double beds, he stopped dead in the doorway.

He was going to be spending the night alone in a hotel room with Caitlyn.

So? It would be just like the time they camped out in the backyard and told ghost stories. Right?

Sure it would. Except Bryan wasn't with them. And they were both over the age of ten. And Caitlyn was....

"What's wrong?" She stepped next to him, her fresh scent going right to his head. "Is the room okay?"

Caitlyn was beautiful, that's what she was. Golden-haired, bright-eyed, sweet-faced, sexy-shaped... *Back the truck up.* He wasn't going there. Not with his friend's sister. Not with someone who'd been such a good friend to the whole Anderson family.

"Sure. It's great. No problem at all. Um…you hungry? I could really go for a pizza. Or maybe some barbecue. They say it's great in Kansas City."

She peered at him, her eyebrows pulling together in a perplexed frown. It made a crease in her forehead that he wanted to smooth away. *Hands off, idiot.*

"Are you sure you're okay?"

"Nervous about tomorrow, I guess."

Her face cleared. "Oh, of course. Well, don't worry. Worrying doesn't ever help. Believe me, I know. But we should probably eat right away so we can get to bed early."

"Yes," he said, his voice suddenly thick. *Get to bed early.* Good plan. In those beds that just happened to be right next to each other.

Gulp. Sure, Caitlyn was like a sister, and she'd been a good friend forever…but she also had those gorgeous curves and that sweet, sassy attitude, and he wasn't a freaking monk. She was getting him all wound up, and they'd barely gotten here.

Eyes on the prize, Anderson, he reminded himself. Tryout. Friars. Tomorrow.

CHAPTER THREE

All through their dinner—smoky barbecue ribs that nearly made her faint with pleasure—Caitlyn tried to get back that look in Eli's eyes. The one that had flashed across his face in the hotel room. That look that said, "One night isn't going to be nearly enough for all the things I want to do to you." Had she hallucinated it out of sheer frustrated lust?

Entirely possible. Especially since he was now talking nonstop about her brother Bryan.

Bryan. She loved her brother, but for a moment, she kind of hated him too. If not for Bryan, she wouldn't be anyone's *little sister*. She'd just be a woman.

"You came back to Sapphire Falls because of him, didn't you?" Eli was asking.

"Yes, but that's not the only reason. I love Sapphire Falls. Where else can you walk down the street and know exactly what everyone's favorite kind of candy is?"

"Seriously?"

"Of course! Hailey likes the margarita lime truffles. Lindsay loves the mocha almond fudge. TJ goes for peanut brittle. Mrs. Gunderson can't get enough raspberry ganache."

"What's mine? Bet I have you stumped there."

She narrowed her eyes at him. "No. I have your number. You're a cyborg. What else could possibly explain your complete lack of a sweet tooth?"

He laughed, and she involuntarily pressed her legs together under the table. That rumbly male sound just *did* something to her.

"I like some sweet things," he said, blinking innocently as he popped a piece of cornbread slathered with honey butter into his mouth.

Was he *flirting* with her? Or just teasing her? She didn't

24

even know anymore, that's how flustered he'd gotten her. "You like my chocolate chip cookies," she said weakly. "I've seen you eat a whole dozen."

"I'd have to be dead not to like your chocolate chip cookies." Was that a meaningful glance from those knee-meltingly blue eyes? "But you're right, candy isn't really my thing. Now if more candy had bacon in it, that might be different."

"I consider that a personal challenge." If he couldn't appreciate *her*, maybe he'd appreciate her candy.

"Game on," he answered.

They were so caught up in their conversation that they didn't notice the waiter looming over them until he repeated, loudly, "Dessert?"

Caitlyn burst into giggles, and Eli shook his head "no" to the waiter. He left muttering something about "country kids," which made them laugh all the more. As they waited for the check, Eli cocked his head at her. "Did you like living in Denver? Did you enjoy being a city girl?"

She leaned toward him. "Want to know a secret? I was homesick the entire time. I missed my family. I missed the diner. I used to call my mom for gossip updates. Do you think I'm pathetic?"

His expression softened, his gaze caressing her. "No, you're not pathetic. I love the town too. I'll never forget how everyone helped us out after my dad's stroke. We didn't have to cook a meal for about three months. And there was always someone calling to ask if we needed anything." He shook his head. "I wouldn't want to live anywhere else."

A stubborn little seed of hope blossomed in her heart. A vision flashed into her brain—her and Eli walking down Main Street, pushing a stroller, laughing, gazing into each other's eyes. Another baby hung in a backpack on Eli's back. He looked so happy, all the shadows gone from his face. And she looked great too, even though she had a little baby bump... Three kids and Eli, that's all she really wanted in the world.

She banished the vision before it could take hold and torture her too much. "But what if you get signed? You'll have to go to San Diego. Are you okay with that?"

"Sure." He shrugged. "Baseball careers don't last forever. I wouldn't mind living in Southern California for a while. The beach, the rollerblades, the California girls. You guys could come visit. Once Bryan can travel."

Aaaaaand...there went her happy vision. Another one took its place. In this one, Eli was on rollerblades, falling flat on his face while she laughed her ass off.

"What's so funny?" Eli was asking.

"Oh, nothing. Just thinking about what a talented athlete you are." She smiled at him innocently.

They talked baseball for the rest of the evening. Back in the hotel room, a semi-awkward silence fell between them.

"I'm...uh...going to change in the bathroom," she finally said. "I'm wiped out."

"Good idea," he said quickly. "I'll probably be asleep by the time you're done."

In the bathroom, she took an extra-long time to get control of her nerves. This was silly. She'd spent the night in the same house as Eli back when they were kids. This was no different. Still, she bundled herself up into a pair of pink cupcake-print flannel pajamas that would have been more suitable for January in Nebraska than Kansas in July.

Better safe than tempted.

When she came out of the bathroom, she saw that Eli had had the same thought. He lay on his back wearing sweatpants and a Sapphire Falls Softball League t-shirt, the covers half on, half off. His arm lay across his eyes, as if he was trying to block the light—or maybe the sight of her. "You can turn off the light whenever you're ready," he told her.

She crawled into her bed, pulled the covers all the way

to her chin, and turned off the light on the nightstand. "Good night."

"'Night," he mumbled.

A hushed quiet fell over the darkened room. Too much quiet. The sound of Eli's breathing made her too restless to sleep. She kept imagining his broad chest rising and falling, his long legs stretched all the way past the foot of the bed.

She tossed and turned, finally deciding it was simply too hot in the room for her favorite pajamas. Carefully, she reached under the covers and removed her pajama bottoms. She sighed, stretching out her legs and wiggling her toes. That was better.

She closed her eyes, then opened one when she heard rustling from Eli's bed. Peering through the darkness, she saw a pale flash of fabric—he was dropping his t-shirt to the floor next to the bed.

He must have had the same idea. Now they were both half-dressed, and her heart was pounding in her throat. Did he know she'd also stripped down? Did he care? She waited, tense and quivering, for his next move.

He gave a soft snore.

God, she was stupid. Like he'd even notice if she stripped entirely naked and danced across the carpet.

Fine. She pulled off her pajama top. Underneath it, she wore a thin camisole—no wonder she was so hot. Why the heck had she overdressed to the point of suffocation? If Eli was going to be oblivious to her existence, she might as well be comfortable.

What the hell was Caitlyn doing? Trying to kill him? Was she now completely naked over there? He went hard as a rock at the thought. *Fuck.* He wasn't supposed to get a hard-on in the presence of his friend's sister. But even her ridiculous fuzzy pink pj's couldn't hide those amazing

curves, and damn, he was only human. He shifted
uncomfortably, the sweatpants rubbing against his cock. He
usually slept naked, or at the most in his boxers. He felt
suffocated by all that fabric.

This was never going to work. He listened to make sure
Caitlyn was asleep, and when he didn't hear any sound
from her direction, he slid off his sweatpants and dropped
them on top of his shirt. Ahhhh, that was better. Maybe
now he had a chance of catching some zzzz's before the
main event tomorrow.

As long as he didn't think too much about Caitlyn over
there naked, her nightclothes in a little pile by her bed, just
like his. It was kind of funny, if you thought about it.

Smiling, he drifted off.

In the middle of the night, the urge to visit the bathroom
dragged him from a deep sleep. Blinking in the darkness,
he stumbled out of bed. Still mostly asleep, he made his
way across the room toward the bathroom. He yawned
hugely, reaching for the door...

Only to find his arms full of warm, naked flesh. Female
flesh.

Arousal ripped through him, and he dragged the
tempting armful closer against his chest. He buried his nose
in soft hair, ran his hands down curves that cried out to be
touched.

His cock rose again, twice as hard as before. The
woman in his arms trembled, pressed her hips against him.
Nipples perked through her thin top, scraping against his
chest, and oh my God, she wore the tiniest scrap of nothing
in the way of panties. He could rip those things off her with
one flick of his thumb. He could pin her against the wall
and pull those fine legs around his hips and drive his cock
into her—

A soft inhale broke the fantasy.

Horror rushing through him, he dropped the woman
back to the floor.

No, not "the woman." *Caitlyn.* He'd nearly taken Caitlyn Murray up against a wall in a random hotel room in Kansas City. Even now, his erection was nestled against her, as if that part of his body refused to let her go.

"I'm sorry," he mumbled, placing her firmly at arm's length.

"It's…it's okay." She sounded awfully breathless. "I should have turned the light on, but I didn't want to wake you, and…it was my fault. I'm sorry."

"Yeah, but that's no excuse for me mauling you in the middle of the night. I was half asleep and didn't exactly…ah hell, that sounds even worse. I'm really sorry, Caitlyn. It won't happen again. Do you trust me?"

She didn't answer for a moment, and he wished to God he could see her face. Just how angry was she?

"Go to sleep, Eli." It was hard to miss the irritation in her voice. Well, that answered that. She was plenty angry. When he got back to Sapphire Falls, Bryan and Ty would probably beat his ass. And he'd deserve it. Not even a full night had passed in Caitlyn's company and he'd lost his mind.

৩৯৵৶

For a wild, dreamy moment, Caitlyn had thought all her secret fantasies were about to come true. Wrapped in Eli's arms, his firm muscles surrounding her, the scent of his skin had gone right to her head. Hot desire had swept through her entire body. She'd wanted to lick his chest, kiss her way down his body, drop to her knees and lick his hard length. It had felt like every crazy daydream, every nighttime craving rolled into one.

Instead, here she was, even further from what she wanted. Now he *felt bad*, as if he'd accidentally forced something on her that she didn't want. How could she tell him that she'd loved every second, after he'd basically blamed his actions on being too asleep to know what he was doing?

Grrrr. She flopped into bed and pulled her pillow over her head. Now if she could just get her heart to stop its jumping jacks and her pulse to settle down, she could work on her game face for tomorrow.

Note to self for tomorrow: *say nothing. Pretend it never happened. Keep your cool. Just get him to that tryout.*

As it happened, the next morning Eli's extreme case of nerves made it easy to avoid referring to the half-naked incident. When Caitlyn got out of the shower, fully and carefully dressed, he'd already gone to the breakfast buffet and tanked up on coffee. He brought her a cup with plenty of creamers and sugar, as well as a plate of blueberry muffins. She poured creamer in her coffee while he paced around the room.

"Maybe you should go for a jog," she suggested.

"Might pull a muscle," he said tensely. "Or get lost."

She laughed. "Did you eat anything?"

"Nope. Might throw up."

"But you drank some coffee?"

"Little bit." He drummed his fingers on his leg, which couldn't seem to stay still. "You ready to go yet? I want to check out the stadium."

"Eli." She walked over to him and put her hands on his shoulders. She felt the contours of his muscles under the jersey and got momentarily distracted. The power that lurked in his body was enough to make a girl weak in the knees. She forced the memory of last night out of her mind. "This is what you were meant to do. It's going to be fine. Just believe in yourself. I believe in you."

"You do?"

"One hundred percent, without a doubt. Now let's go, before your head explodes."

His reluctant laugh was balm to her soul. At least she could still make him laugh. At least she could still be his friend. Calm him down. Be there for him during such a key moment in his life. Maybe that one brush with nakedness hadn't ruined everything.

She drove him to the nearby campus of the Kansas City Community College. The parking lot by the athletic field was already filled with cars. Young men in baseball uniforms of every variety were making their way toward the field, armed with gym bags and baseball gloves. She whistled at the sight.

"How many people come to these tryouts?"

"Doesn't matter," said Eli tensely, staring out the window. "It's not a competition."

"It's not?"

"Nope. It's not like they're going to pick the top ten or something. They only pick the guys they think have the potential to help the team. Some tryouts, no one gets a call. Most, actually."

"Really? All these people and no one's good enough for them?" Caitlyn pulled into a spot. "Can I watch?"

He shrugged. "It might get kind of boring. Usually the pitchers go last. Until I get to go, you'll be watching a bunch of guys run the sixty-yard dash."

"Doesn't sound too bad to me." Caitlyn gave him a cheeky wink as she hopped out of the Focus. "They'll be wearing baseball pants, right?"

He glared at her. Ooh, had she made Eli just the tiniest bit jealous? Or was it just a general glare based on nerves and tension? She grinned to herself as he slammed her car door and slung his gym bag over his shoulder. He definitely looked even crabbier than he had before.

"I think the sign-up is that-away." She pointed to a long folding table where a few men in warmup jackets were handing out index cards to the shifting line of baseball wannabes. "I'll find a seat on the bleachers. I'll be watching, so knock 'em dead."

She gave him a wave as she headed across the parking

lot.

"That's it?" he called after her. "That's all I get?"

Turning back, she saw him striding toward her, an intent focus in his gaze.

"The least you could do is give me a kiss for good luck." He swept her into his arms and planted a kiss full on her mouth.

She tasted coffee and five-alarm heat. The shock of it vibrated all the way to her toes. She didn't even get a chance to really kiss him back before he plopped her back down on the pavement.

His blue eyes gleaming, he spun around and headed for the sign-up line.

She pressed her lips together, still tasting the warm force of his mouth. Why had he done that? Just to mess with her? Keep her from ogling hot outfielders?

As soon as she'd caught her breath and found a seat in the bleachers, she extracted her cell phone and fired off a text.

Seriously? You call that a kiss? Your moves need work, big shot.

She saw the exact moment when he got the text. He clutched his chest as if she'd shot him, and pretended to nearly fall to his knees. Then he texted back.

Challenge accepted.

CHAPTER FOUR

Thank God for Caitlyn. Her light teasing relaxed Eli enough so he could focus on the tryout. He couldn't think about why he'd decided to kiss her, or how her lips had felt in that brief, scorching moment. He definitely couldn't dwell on her critique of his "moves." This was one of the biggest moments in his life. So he shoved all thoughts of her out of his mind and concentrated on the drills taking place on the field.

After he signed in and got his card—he was officially number 52 until the end of the tryout—he stood around with the other pitching candidates along the sidelines. It was a hot, sultry day, with an achingly blue sky and no breeze whatsoever. But you'd never know it from the way the players ran and jumped and dove for grounders. Some of them were so young and energetic; it made him want to cry. But a few were his age or even older.

The first drill was a sixty-yard dash. Everyone ran two sprints, and anyone who took longer than seven seconds was sent home.

Eli watched the first cut leave with deep sympathy. Imagine coming all that way and not making it past the first test. Good thing he was a pitcher, because he hadn't been practicing his sprints at all. Even so, he was almost tempted to see if he'd make the cut, if just to show off in front of Caitlyn.

Don't go there, idiot. Stay focused.

After the sprinting, the outfielders got their turn. They each fielded five balls—a mix of fly balls and grounders— and then threw to home base. Many of them fired off some real rockets, others fell short. Eli spotted a radar gun trained on the harder-throwing guys. Excitement clenched his gut. That same radar gun would be timing his speed when his turn came.

When the outfielders were done, it was time for the infielders and a rapid-fire sequence of grounders down the line of prospects. It was fun to watch, though the skill level was all over the place. Eli realized he had no need to worry about making a fool of himself. He could out-field some of these guys with his arm in a cast.

Then again, he reminded himself, it wasn't a competition. The only thing that mattered was his turn on the mound. Of all the pitches he'd delivered in his life, these would be the only ones that mattered.

After the fielding and catching drills came batting practice. Again, only a certain number were called to stay for that; the rest went home. Eli felt the tension rise, especially among the pitchers. Their turn was coming. Finally, halfway through batting practice, a scout came over and told them how their bullpen sessions would work.

"We'll take you one by one, in order of your number, so pay attention to when you're up. Miss your number, you're out. Make sure you're nice and loose, 'cause you get about fifteen pitches once you're on the mound. Get a catcher to help you warm up, or catch for each other, whatever works. When you're on the mound, pitch what the scout calls for. He's looking for certain things, so don't get cute. Just do what he says. You got ten minutes before we call the first guy." He wheeled away, clipboard in hand.

Hell. They didn't even get to call their own pitches. That sucked for Eli, because while he had a strong fastball and a decent curve, his knuckleball really set him apart. Would he even get to throw it?

Trying not to be discouraged, Eli caught the eye of one of the catchers, who nodded back. They set up on the sidelines and played a little catch, nice and easy. Eli didn't watch the other pitchers, instead focusing on the ball, the glove, his shoulder, his mechanics, letting his body get warm and loose. The only time he got distracted was when he caught a glimpse of the scout with the radar gun taking a water break.

And talking to Caitlyn, who had moved down to the front row.

In her jeans and pink top, a baseball cap holding back her ponytail, she looked cute as a kitten, and he wasn't the only one who noticed. The scout seemed to be showing her how the radar gun worked while she smiled admiringly.

Only Caitlyn, thought Eli. Only Caitlyn could waltz into a baseball tryout and have a scout eating out of her hand. She hadn't even brought any of her candy—it was her sheer sweetness and charm that did it.

Well, screw the knuckleball. He could make it without that one pitch. He'd have to pitch his heart out, that was all.

When they called number 52, he was ready, although his heart felt as if it might take a swan dive right into the dirt. He strolled onto the mound, using the short walk to calm his breathing. He settled into place, kicking the dirt the way he liked it. The catcher threw him the ball, and he looked to the side, to the scout. Beyond him, he saw Caitlyn perched on the very edge of the bench, looking extremely nervous. Her hands were gripped together, her gaze fixed on him, her body taut.

She was nervous. For him. The sweetness of that thought made a sense of calm settle over him. Calm and protectiveness. All he wanted to do now was make Caitlyn feel better. To do that…well, he had the power right there in his hands. A baseball.

He could do anything with that baseball. Write his own future. Change his world. Make Caitlyn happy.

The scout gave the sign for a fastball. Done. Eli went into his windup and reared back, putting every bit of his tension and desire and power into that pitch.

Wham. It hit the glove perfectly, even causing the catcher to flinch a tiny bit.

Two more fastballs, then some breaking balls, then more fastballs. A changeup. Eli threw on command, whatever the scout called, giving it his all. He lost count of the pitches—it didn't matter anyway. They all had to be his best. And they were. The only question was, would his best be good enough?

The head scout conferred with the other scout, the one with the radar gun. From the expression on his face, Eli guessed that he hadn't set any records with his speed. No big surprise there. His fastball was strong but not exactly world-class. His stomach sank. There it went, his dream, floating away like infield dust in a wind gust.

But the radar gun scout was now saying something else, something that made the head scout cock his head. He turned to Eli.

"Number fifty-two, you get one more pitch. You got anything we haven't seen yet?"

For a moment Eli didn't understand. Then it sank in. They were asking *him* for a pitch selection.

"Knuckleball," he croaked, almost afraid to say the word aloud. "I got a pretty good knuckleball."

"All right. Let's see it."

Be a good one, Eli prayed as he settled the ball between his thumb and the first joints of his index and middle finger. He loved this pitch, because it did whatever the hell it wanted, moved up and down, all over the place, completely unpredictable.

Kind of like life, in his experience. One minute you were in college, the next your father had a stroke. One minute you were on the way to baseball stardom, the next you were ringing up a case of flat-head screws. Life was a freaking knuckleball, and the more you accepted that, the better off you'd be.

Even now, his knuckleball might decide to desert him. You just never knew.

But it didn't. Instead, it danced and fluttered its way to the plate with its usual crazy randomness, then dropped into the pitcher's glove smack in the lower third of the strike zone. Confounding and unhittable.

"Try that one again," called the scout.

So Eli did it again. Different crazy dance, same conclusion: strike. He heard a low whistle coming from someone, and a "what the hell" from someone else.

"Again."

He'd definitely gone past his fifteen pitches, but who was he to object? He threw several more knuckleballs, until the scouts were satisfied and nodded him off the mound.

No one said much to him as he walked off the diamond in a daze. No one else had been asked to throw extra pitches. Was that a good thing or a bad thing? With his thoughts whirling, he went back to the sidelines. One of the players still waiting his turn glanced his way with a smirk.

"Knuckleball, huh? Thanks for the trip down memory lane."

Another pitcher, a guy who'd thrown in the upper 80s, snickered. "Thought it went out with sideburns and bell bottoms."

Eli didn't answer, but his heart sank right to the pit of his stomach. The guy had a point. Who cared about knuckleballs anymore? It was a dying pitch. Only about two active major leaguers could be considered true knuckleballers. No one in the Bigs cared whether you could throw it or not. Maybe instead of showing off his stuff, he'd made a fool of himself.

He'd probably provided the scouts with a funniest story of the year. Later tonight, they'd toss back a few beers while they howled with laughter at the idiot who'd showed up at a major league tryout and thrown a sixty-mile-an-hour knuckleball. He stole a glance at Caitlyn, wondering if she realized what a disaster this was.

Apparently not—she looked ready to burst with excitement. She danced up and down as she gave him two big thumbs up.

He shook that off with a doubtful shrug. Maybe she

didn't understand enough about baseball to know what had just happened. Not likely, though. Caitlyn had always been a huge baseball fan.

She beckoned him over with an impatient gesture.

With a feeling of dread—he didn't want to explain how stupid he'd just looked—he made his way over to her spot in the bleachers. As soon as he came close enough, she leaned over the railing and threw her arms around him. "You were amazing. Definitely the best one here. No contest," she whispered in his ear.

Her warmth made him feel a little bit better. "You saw it all?"

"Of course I did. I took some videos for everyone back home, too."

Videos. Videos of him throwing junk before a Friars scout. But it wasn't her fault. He couldn't take his disappointment out on her.

"Good thinking," he made himself mutter, then set her back on her feet. Holding her in his arms was too confusing, anyway. It felt too good, much better than it ought to. "I have to stick around in case they decide to call a scrimmage. When do we have to get back home?"

"Well, I have to be at work the day after tomorrow, but your dad says take your time."

"My dad?"

"Yeah, I called your parents right before you pitched. They were listening on the speaker phone. The way things go in Sapphire Falls, probably about twenty people were listening in. Everyone's so proud of you, Eli."

Oh for crap's sake. He could just picture everyone huddled over the phone, listening to nothing more than the thud of a ball in a glove. And then the unforgettable moment when the scout asked the fateful question, *You got anything we haven't seen yet?*

"It's just a tryout, Caitlyn. I don't want everyone getting all excited over nothing."

"Shh. It's not nothing. It doesn't matter if you get the call or not. You came out here and did your best."

Good God, what was this, kindergarten?

Finally, his frustration burst through his control. "You don't know what you're talking about. I made a huge mistake throwing those knuckleballs. I should have stuck with the heat. That's all they want in the major leagues. I don't know why they asked for more pitches, anyway."

"That's crazy! Your knuckleball is not a mistake! It's your best pitch."

"My best pitch barely cracks seventy miles an hour. What a joke."

"But it's not supposed to. Knuckleballs don't rely on speed, you know that. The scouts know that, too."

"What do you mean?"

"Well, I got talking with Stewart, the guy with the radar gun. He works with Crush Taylor, the Playboy Pitcher, can you believe it? Crush owns the Kilby Catfish now, and I guess the Friars like getting his feedback on new talent. When he can't come to tryouts himself, he sends Stewart. Anyway, I told him that you're a legend in Sapphire Falls because of your knuckleball. I guaranteed he'd never see a crazier pitch than that one. At first he thought I didn't know what I was talking about. But I told him that I saw R.A. Dickey pitch both before and after he learned the knuckleball that earned him the Cy Young Award, and after that he listened to me."

He drew away, staring at her with dropped jaw. "So it was your doing? Them asking if I had any other pitches?"

"Well, it was just a conversation. I also told him about my homemade Cracker Jacks. He said he's going to call the shop and place an order, but if they sign you, I just might comp him a whole order."

"Caitlyn—" He ripped off his baseball cap and swiped his hand across the back of his sweat-damp head. "I can't believe…why did you…why were you even talking to him?" *This wasn't her fault, this wasn't her fault*, he reminded himself.

"Why are you so worried?" Huge and soft, her hazel eyes showed nothing but innocent good intentions. He felt like an ass for all the anger coursing through him. "Isn't it better to show them everything you're capable of? You threw lots of fastballs and curve balls too."

"Yeah, but you know what's going to stick in their minds? Sixty-miles-an-hour junk, that's what."

"Eli!"

"I better get back," he mumbled, stalking away before he said anything worse to her. It wasn't Caitlyn's fault that she was a sweet girl who liked to talk to people, and that people adored her. It wasn't her fault he'd thrown those pitches. This was on him. *He'd* screwed up his last shot at his dream. No one else.

With his back to Caitlyn, Eli watched the rest of the prospects take their fifteen shots at destiny. No one else got a request for extra pitches. No one else threw a knuckleball.

Nope, that claim to fame was all his.

CHAPTER FIVE

Caitlyn's entire right thumbnail was bitten down past the tip and her stomach was in knots by the time Eli exited the field at the end of the tryout.

Had she messed up? She hadn't even intended to talk to the scout but they were both standing there and both, clearly, interested in what was going on and she'd mentioned that she was a friend of Eli's, that they were both from Sapphire Falls... She frowned. That's how conversations went. One person said something and then the other said something in return and the topic went from there. Stewart was a nice guy. She hadn't done anything wrong.

Except that Eli had looked so frustrated. That irritated set to his mouth with the worry in his eyes and the tension through his shoulders had made her stomach hurt. He'd been so great and she wanted *him* to feel that.

She wanted to take him in her arms and hug him and rub his back and tell him that she thought he was amazing for so much more than his knuckleball. She wanted to kiss him and tell him that she could name two dozen things she loved about him that had nothing to do with baseball.

But none of that would matter. She was just Caitlyn. Eli's friend's little sister. She knew he liked her and cared—enough to help her buy a new car, for instance—but her believing in him, and telling him that he could never throw another pitch in his life and she'd still be madly in love with him, wouldn't matter.

And she *was* in love with him. That seemed clearer than ever as she'd sat watching his tryout.

Sure, the tight pants and his wide shoulders and the incredible power in his body when he coiled and released on each pitch made her hot and itchy. But it was the determined look on his face, the focused concentration, the way he'd looked so satisfied when his fastball hit square and the pleasure when he'd thrown that first knuckleball that made her heart swell.

She wanted this for him. She wanted him happy above all else.

And that's when she realized that she was in trouble.

On the very off chance that he *didn't* get the call—because crazy stuff happened all the time in baseball—she was going to be as devastated as Eli would be. But if he *did* get the call, that would take him away from her, potentially all the way to San Diego. That would be pretty damned devastating too.

Being in love kind of sucked.

Eli approached the bleachers where she was sitting and Caitlyn made herself paste on a big smile and bounce up from her seat.

Her job here was cheerleader. She had to make him feel good about this tryout, no matter the outcome. He didn't want to hear about how much she appreciated his easy smile or his sense of humor or how much her heart melted every time she saw him with his dad. This wasn't about how she felt.

"That was awesome," she said, coming down the four steps to the bottom of the bleachers. She hopped down to the dirt and grinned up at him. "Let's go celebrate."

Eli gave her a frown. "There's nothing to celebrate yet. There might not be at all."

She tamped down the urge to grab him and shake him. "You tried out," she said. "That's huge, Eli. You took a step toward your dream. And you came out here and gave it your all. That's worth celebrating."

He shoved a hand through his hair. "Nah. I just want a shower and then maybe we should hit the road."

"Hit the road?" she repeated. "Go home? Now? It's four o'clock. By the time we get all packed up and shower and eat, we won't get to Sapphire Falls until after midnight."

He shrugged. "I should get back. No reason to stay. And I'll need to get back to the store and stuff."

Now Caitlyn let her eyes narrow. "We're not going home."

"What?"

"I mean tonight. We're not leaving. We're going out."

"Out?"

She nodded. "Out."

She pulled her keys from her pocket and started for the parking lot. Ten steps later she glanced back. "You coming?"

He looked annoyed, but she didn't care. She knew Eli. He had a lot of friends and, of course, spent time at the local Sapphire Falls events and hung at the Come Again on Friday nights with everyone else. It wasn't like he never had a good time. But he didn't let loose, he didn't let go, he was never more than a mile or two from the store and his family. He was amazingly loyal and responsible.

He needed a night off.

And she was just the girl to give it to him.

He pulled his bag up higher on his shoulder and followed her to the car.

He threw his bag into the backseat and looked at her over the top of the car. "Where are we—"

"Don't worry about it," she said. "I've got this." She got into the car and started the engine.

"What do you have, exactly?" he asked, getting in next to her.

"Tonight," she said, backing out and turning the car toward the hotel. "I've got tonight covered."

Eli didn't say anything to that and Caitlyn barely kept from grinning. He wasn't good at giving up control, she knew. He'd taken over with his family, the store, everything. He let his dad think that Chip was still making some decisions, but the truth was, Eli was keeping it all

43

going.

Well, tonight, he needed to trust her.

She pulled up in front of the hotel, put the car into park and looked at her watch. "Okay, you have fifteen minutes to get cleaned up. Then you need to be back down here."

He lifted an eyebrow. "For what?"

She wasn't sure. Fun. That was all she knew. She had fifteen minutes to figure it out. "You'll see."

Twelve minutes later, Eli was out of the room, his hair damp, a sexy day's worth of stubble on his jaw. He was back in jeans and a simple blue t-shirt that brought out his eyes and made her sigh.

But this was about being a cheerleader, not a drooling fangirl.

"Now what?" he asked, spreading his arms wide.

God, those shoulders, and that chest, and those abs...

She shook her head and gave him a smile. "We can walk. Let's go."

While he'd been showering and changing, she'd scoped out fun local bars. Then thought better of it. She didn't know Kansas City and even with GPS, she didn't want to worry about getting them back to the hotel. Plus, she needed a drink. She had an edge to take off too.

Thinking about Eli and what it would mean for him, and everyone else, if he got the call, what it would mean if he didn't get the call, why she was really here, all of the things she really wanted to say to him but knew she couldn't, had her so wound up she didn't know how she was going to keep up the charade of good-friend-and-chauffeur-only for another twenty-four hours or so.

Bottom line—she wanted them to *both* relax and have fun.

So they were going to *walk* the two blocks to the closest bar.

Eli fell into step beside her as she started east across the parking lot.

"Sorry I was an ass at the tryout," he said after a few minutes.

She looked over. He had his hands tucked into the front pockets of his jeans.

"I'm sorry I got everyone on the phone. Or that I talked to the scout. Whatever you're upset about."

He gave her a sideways smile. "How about both?"

She rolled her eyes. "Fine. Both. Sorry, I was trying to be supportive."

He bumped her shoulder with his. A friendly gesture he'd done a million times in her life. And her heart dropped a bit. It was a *friendly* gesture. As were all the other gestures and words and looks and smiles he'd ever given her.

Except for the delicious groping in the dark last night in the bathroom doorway.

Her body heated at the memory and she swallowed hard.

"It means a lot that you're here," he finally said.

She laughed lightly. "Like I gave you a choice."

She led him up the walk to the front door of *Eddie's*, the bar and grill she'd found on her phone while she waited for him. It didn't look bad. The parking lot was about half full and well lit, all the bulbs in the sign worked, and the familiar aroma of burgers and fried food made her stomach rumble.

Eli pulled the door open for her. "Honestly," he said as she passed him. "I much preferred your good-luck kiss to the ones I would've gotten from Ty and Bryan."

She snorted, surprised by his banter. "Like *you* gave *me* a choice on that one."

He moved in behind her as she stopped inside the door and surveyed the room.

"Yeah, what was that about?" he asked.

She glanced up at him. "What do you mean?"

"I had to *take* my good-luck kiss? Shouldn't you have

45

been *giving* it to me?"

Caitlyn tried to study his face but a shadow fell just right so that she couldn't discern the emotion in his eyes. But he had to be teasing her. Surely.

"Are you going to try to tell me that you didn't do as well as you wanted to because of that kiss?" she asked lightly.

He shrugged. "I prefer to blame my performance on anything *but* myself."

She knew that wasn't true. Eli was a hard worker, no matter what work he was doing, and was his own harshest critic. He would never try to excuse anything he did.

"I'm not talking about the tryout anymore until I've had a shot of Jäger," she said, turning away.

The bartender caught her eye and waved her in, indicating they could sit wherever they wanted to. Caitlyn headed for a tall round table for two along the wall across from the bar.

"Jäger?" Eli asked, taking the stool across from her.

The table was small and with his long legs, his knees bumped hers as they both got comfortable. Even after a few seconds of shifting and turning, Caitlyn had to accept the fact that their legs where going to be touching throughout their dinner.

"Jäger. Definitely."

He shook his head. "Even after New Year's?"

She didn't love the taste of Jägermeister, but she did love the buzz it gave her. Typically she stuck with sweeter, fruitier drinks, even shots. Butterscotch schnapps, peppermint schnapps, peach schnapps—really anything with "schnapps" at the end. But when she wanted a quick, warm buzz, Jäger was her go to.

She knew Eli liked it too.

"Especially after New Year's," she said.

The New Year's party in Sapphire Falls was one of many holiday traditions—hell, it was one of many

46

traditions period. Sapphire Falls loved their festivals and parties and customs. The New Year's party started at the community center with a band and a dance and tons of food, potluck of course. Then, around eleven-thirty, everyone made their way to the town square—regardless of the weather. They had hot chocolate and hot cider and coffee and everyone snuck in their favorite spirit to add to the cups. Though since everyone did it, and everyone knew that everyone did it, she wasn't so sure that it was really "sneaking."

They all gathered around the tall homemade replica of the tower and ball in New York's Times Square as they counted down the minutes to the new year. Then, cliché or not, they all sang *Auld Lang Syne* and kissed their dates.

And anyone else who would pucker up.

Which was why Eli was asking.

She and some friends had taken Jägermeister in their flasks and had started tipping it back early. Her rationale had been sound—it had been freezing cold this past year and peppermint schnapps in cocoa just wasn't going to cut it.

Consequently, she'd kissed Tim Watkins. Three times. And they hadn't been pecks. Tim, who'd had a crush on her since the sixth grade, had recognized that she was…ahem…feeling *friendlier* than usual and had taken full advantage.

The photo of her being dipped back and full-on, open-mouth-with-tongue kissed had run on the front page of the Sapphire Falls paper and was the first photo that popped up on the town's website under "Winter Fun."

"Especially after New Year's?" Eli repeated, eyebrow up. "Tim made you rethink your stance on dating smug bigots who can't keep their mouths shut?" He tipped his head. "I think I got that quote right. That's what you called him in ninth grade when you declared he better not ever get within five feet of you or you'd knee him in the balls, right?"

Caitlyn felt her cheeks heat and her grin spread at the same time. "He was a bully and an idiot who had been picking on Melissa Cotter when I said that," she said. "But he was definitely within five feet of you on New Year's," Eli reminded her.

"Yes," she nodded. She regretted that. Not because the kissing had been bad. Apparently even big-mouthed smug bigots could turn into decent kissers. But because Tim was still a bully and an idiot. She gave Eli a smile. "But so was Wade Frederick."

"You kissed Wade too?"

"And a couple of others. And Wade kissed *me*, by the way."

Eli leaned in. "I didn't see you kiss Wade on New Year's."

She frowned. "So? You think you saw everyone I kissed?"

"Yes. I mean, I…well, I think… Bryan would have noticed."

Caitlyn watched Eli stumble over his words, warmth spreading through her. "You were paying attention to who I was kissing?" she asked.

"I…" He sighed. "Apparently not as closely as I thought."

"You were watching on purpose?" She wasn't sure what to think about all of this.

Eli didn't respond right away, but after a few seconds he met her gaze directly and said, "I was trying to decide if I could get away with stealing one from you myself. Figured New Year's was the perfect opportunity."

It would have been. Anything went when everyone was tipsy and huddled close in the always-cold mid-winter air. "But you didn't," she pointed out.

"No."

"Why not?"

He hesitated and Caitlyn held her breath. Maybe he—
"Tim was kind of monopolizing you," he said with a
half-smile. "And you weren't pushing him away."

Okay, he was going to joke about it. Fine. She
grimaced. "Yeah. Maybe Jäger is a bad idea." She grabbed
one of the menus leaning against the wall behind the
ketchup bottle.

"You think you might end up kissing someone you'll
regret?"

Her head came up. Was he teasing? Joking? Fishing?
Suddenly she was tired of wondering.

"I figure if you won't kiss me even when you've been
drinking and have the perfect excuse, then I'm not too
worried about anything happening between us tonight,
Jäger or not."

His jaw tensed for a moment and she saw his fingers
grip the menu he held tighter. Then his eyes narrowed.
"Then let's do Jäger shots. If we have nothing to worry
about, what the hell?"

He was challenging her? Really? "Fine." She'd take the
dare.

He gave their order to the waitress—four shots of Jäger
and two beers—and told her they'd also be ordering food
after they looked over the menus.

Caitlyn tried not to study him.

But geez, he needed to *relax*. Maybe more so now. She
wasn't looking at him and she could swear she could *feel*
the tension coming off of him. Good grief. She'd always
thought of Eli as pretty laid-back. He was focused and
driven and responsible to a fault and...

Her thought trailed off. Why had she thought he was
laid-back? He really wasn't. He was friendly and had a
quick smile and everyone liked him, but that didn't mean
he was blasé. That was Bryan. Bryan had always been the
good-time guy, the party guy, the go-big-or-go-home guy.
Ty Bennett too. Ty was more disciplined than Bryan and

had a scary-intense focus when it came to training but he worked hard and *played* hard.

Eli wasn't like that. She glanced at him over the top of her menu. He was studying the food options with a glare.

Yeah, he wasn't carefree. Not even a little bit.

The waitress brought their drinks and took their food order. Caitlyn was going for the grilled chicken sandwich and fries while Eli wanted the sirloin, baked potato and salad. As soon as the other woman moved off, he lifted a shot glass, the look in his eyes a clear challenge.

Caitlyn did the same. "To the start of your incredible baseball career," she said, before he could make a toast.

He shook his head. "No."

She frowned. "Yes. This is the beginning of great things, I can feel it."

He refrained from clinking his glass against hers and shot the black-licorice flavored liqueur back.

She sighed and did the same.

He took a long draw of beer. "So you have a thing for Wade."

She did not have a thing for Wade. Wade was good looking and a great New Year's Eve kisser. But she did not have a thing for him. Because she had a thing for Eli. A big, oh-shit-this-isn't-good thing that made other men pale in comparison.

Come to think of it—having Eli leave Sapphire Falls would actually be a *good* thing. A really good thing. She could actually pay some attention to the other great guys in town and not constantly hold them up against her ideal man. Because said ideal man would be in California.

As the burn from the liquor spread from her stomach out to her extremities and, most importantly, her head. Yes, Eli in California would accomplish so many great things. He'd have the career he'd dreamed of and deserved and *she* would be able to move on.

"I can't wait until you get that phone call," she told

him. She took a big drink of beer and swallowed. "I'm so going to say 'told you so' when you do."

"Stop it."

"I'm serious. Your tryout was great. You're going to get it."

"No way. And stop getting my hopes up."

She frowned. "Well, where are hopes supposed to be? Tamped down under your pillow? Hidden in your sock drawer? Tucked in your back pocket? Hopes are supposed to be *up*, Eli. Up in front of you, leading your way."

He was staring at her. She licked her lip wondering if she had something on it. But she'd only been drinking so far.

"What?" she asked

"You're kind of amazing, you know that?"

Caitlyn felt her eyes widen. "What?"

"You're so optimistic, so positive. Jesus, it's nearly impossible not to believe everything you say."

She couldn't help but grin at that. "Well, good."

"And you're sweet and bubbly and…you really want this for me, don't you? Like *for me*."

She wrinkled her nose. What was he talking about? "Well…*yeah*. We're friends. I want you to have whatever you want."

Strangely, that didn't seem to make him feel better.

"Makes it worse," he muttered and took his second shot.

"Hey."

He set his shot glass down. "Sorry. I just meant—"

"No," she cut him off. "You need to listen to me right now. You were *good* today, Eli. Really good. The best pitcher out there."

"You're biased."

She nodded. "I am. But that doesn't matter. You were good whether I wanted you to be or not."

He searched her eyes. "You really think so?"

"I know so. You were amazing. Not only did you throw well but you were calm and collected, focused, intent. It was very se—*obvious*...that you were giving it your all."

"It was very se?" he repeated, one eyebrow up.

Dammit. She'd almost said sexy. Because it had been that. It had most definitely been that.

"Obvious," she repeated. "It was very *obvious*."

She also became very aware of something she'd been trying to ignore. Her left knee was wedged between *his* knees and her right was pressed between his left leg and the wall. And she didn't want to move an inch. His legs were solid and warm and she wanted nothing more than to press against even more of his solid, warm parts.

He apparently decided to let her comment go and Caitlyn tried to hold back her relief. If she made it back to Sapphire Falls without making Eli completely, irrevocably aware of her feelings for him, she was treating herself to a mani-pedi, because *that* would be a hell of an accomplishment.

"You really saw R.A. Dickey pitch?" Eli asked a moment later.

Surprised by the question, she nodded. "Really did."

"Knuckleball's your favorite pitch?" he asked.

She smiled in spite of the strangeness of the question. "No way, I like the heat best. Fastball right down the middle every time."

Slowly he grinned. "So you're not just blowing sunshine up my skirt with all of this talk about the knuckleball."

"If your knuckleball sucked, I'd tell you."

He reached over the small table and tucked a strand of hair behind her ear.

She'd had no idea that her earlobe was connected to her breasts, but as his finger brushed the lobe, her nipples tightened.

"So you really do think I did okay today?"

"You did *amazingly* today," she assured him.

"I want to believe it."

"What can I do to help you believe it?"

"Look me in the eye and tell me something I *didn't* do well."

Well, if that's what he needed... She thought back over the day. But it was tough. The heat from where her knee was pressed between his traveled up her thigh to the spot that had been secretly aching for him ever since bumping into him in the bathroom doorway last night. Then there were those piercing blue eyes boring into hers.

"Okay, third pitch," she said, replaying it in her mind. "You released too late."

He nodded. "I did."

"And on the eighth pitch, you didn't stride out as far as you should have."

His eyes narrowed. "Okay."

"And there was one..." She thought back. "Maybe like twelve, where you—"

"Okay," Eli cut in. "Got it. I made some mistakes."

She started shaking her head. "No. You had the best tryout of the day. If they don't sign you they're crazy. Because *in spite* of those *minor* things, you were throwing hard and accurate and—"

The waitress arrived with their plates just then.

"I'm going to hit the restroom."

Eli slid off the stool, his legs tangling with hers for a moment, before he got free and stood.

Caitlyn watched him retreat and felt like a complete failure in the area of cheerleader and general supportive friend.

She picked up a fry and nibbled on it, but her appetite had disappeared. Instead she reached for her second shot and tipped it back. Then she reached for her phone.

A moment later her brother picked up. "Hey, how'd it go?"

"He did great."

"Sounded like it," Bryan agreed.

"You heard?"

"We all heard. We were with Chip. I made my famous cheese dip."

Caitlyn grinned. Of course Sapphire Falls had turned Eli's tryout into a party. She loved that. This tryout wasn't just about Eli's family—it was about everyone who loved him and knew he deserved this.

"Well, he doesn't think so," she said.

"You gotta convince him."

"I'm trying. I was wondering…what would you do if you were here?"

She wasn't just failing Eli here. Bryan had trusted her to get this done because he couldn't. He'd told her "You're my legs, Cait. You gotta get Eli to Kansas City". She didn't think her brother actually realized how his words had stabbed her in the heart.

This whole kidnapping plan was Bryan's idea. It was exactly the kind of thing Bryan loved. He would have made the road trip into some huge adventure and he and Eli and Ty—because of course Ty would have come along—would have gone out on the town tonight and partied and they would have helped Eli forget any doubt about how great he'd done today.

But a truck had crossed the centerline on a mountain road where Ty and Bryan had been biking a little over a year ago, and now Bryan spent part of his time in a wheelchair and all of his time with two legs that didn't do all of the things he needed and wanted them to do anymore. The spinal cord injury was incomplete and Bryan had come a long way in the sixteen months since he'd been thrown down the side of the mountain, but the fact remained that he'd never be one hundred percent. Coming with Eli to Kansas City would have required the wheelchair. Bryan hated the thing, and in the past couple of months had started simply avoiding things that would make him rely on the chair.

It killed her a little bit each time she watched him do something that was harder than it should be or took longer than it used to.

"I'd take him out and get him drunk and laid," Bryan said.

Caitlyn felt her stomach flip. Well, they were working on the first and as for the second...

"But that's probably what I would have done even if he was in a celebratory mood," Bryan said. "I'm sure there are other options."

"Well, we've each already had two shots of Jäger," she said. "So you and I are not totally on different pages."

Bryan chuckled. "Jäger? You? Even after New Year's?"

Caitlyn made a disgusted sound. "You have to admit that Eli is a better option than Tim for Jäger-kissing."

She held her breath. What would Bryan say to that? To even the hint that something could happen between her and Eli?

"Very good point," Bryan replied.

Caitlyn froze. Bryan hadn't freaked out. He hadn't laughed that off. He hadn't said, "I'd fucking kill him."

She frowned. Wasn't that what brothers were supposed to say about their friends and sisters hooking up? Bryan didn't even sound surprised by the idea.

"So take the edge off with the shots and then be the bossy little thing I know you can be. Tell him to knock off the pity party. Tell him he's awesome. Tell him he did great."

"Bossy little thing?"

"Yeah, by the way, I'm not missing that while you're gone."

"I'm only bossy when you need it."

"I'm fine."

She frowned. She wanted to go back to the Eli conversation but couldn't let this go entirely. "No. You're not fine. You're putting on a show for Mom."

Their mother was *not* handling Bryan's accident and disability well. At all. She was in deep denial, actually, and Bryan was allowing it—encouraging it even. To the point where he also acted like everything was fine when he was with her. Which meant he faked a lot when their mom was around.

"Just focus on Eli," Bryan said, sounding very tired suddenly.

But she'd come home to Sapphire Falls to focus on *Bryan*. Her big brother needed help, whether he admitted it or not, and not the "everything's just fine" approach their mother was taking. Bryan needed *her*. Someone who didn't have a spouse or kids or a business or even a demanding, challenging job—no matter how much she wanted all of those things.

Another reason for her to stay unattached to Eli. If Eli was going to stay in Sapphire Falls for good and run the hardware store and make his life in his beloved hometown, then maybe. *Maybe* they could get involved. But as long as Eli's attention and hopes and plans were focused outside of Sapphire Falls, she needed to keep her heart safe. Because she wasn't going anywhere.

"So after I get him mellow with Jäger and tell him he's great, then what?" she asked, letting Bryan steer the conversation back to Eli. She'd already done both of those things. She'd love to know what the next step was.

"You'd be surprised how much a strong shot and a beautiful girl's admiration can do."

She smiled. "Thanks for the compliment. But come on."

"Guys love girls who think they're awesome."

Her heart did a little skip at the word "love". "I do, actually, think he's awesome."

"I know you do."

There was something in Bryan's voice she couldn't quite put her finger on but that made her sit up a little straighter.

"Have fun," Bryan said. "Life's short. You never know what tomorrow might look like."

She felt her heart squeeze hard. No one knew better than Bryan how an entire life could get turned upside down in a second.

"I love you, Bry," she said.

"Ditto."

The moment they disconnected, Caitlyn felt her stool being swiveled. She came face-to-face with Eli.

"Eli, what—"

He cupped the back of her head and covered her mouth with his.

It didn't last long. At least, it didn't last long *enough*, in her opinion. But it was...amazing. Yes, that was definitely the word for the day.

"Did you really memorize each of my tryout pitches?" he asked, resting his forehead against hers.

She nodded, unable to speak. Because she'd also memorized the feel of his lips against hers. And she wanted to keep reliving it.

"Thank you," he said quietly.

"For memorizing them?" she managed to ask.

"For caring."

She melted a little at that. "I can't help it."

She immediately bit her lip. Crap. She had to stop with the slips. On this one she could blame her kiss-muddled brain, but...

Hey, he'd *kissed* her.

"You kissed me," she said softly, pulling back just enough to look up at him.

"I did."

She couldn't help but let her gaze drop to his mouth.

"And I want to do it again."

Her eyes flew back to his.

"There is really something sexy about you knowing all about pitching and every detail of my tryout and believing in me so adamantly."

Oh boy, she really wanted to kiss him again. Or have him kiss her. However, *whatever*, it took to get his mouth on hers.

"Then I overheard you talking to Bryan. You really do think I'm amazing. You aren't just saying that to *me*."

"I've always thought you were amazing," she said.

He pulled her close and lowered his head. "Yeah, the wanting to kiss you isn't new either."

And then he was.

It was so much more than the spontaneous good-luck kiss. It was even more than the one just a minute ago. This one was much more…intentional.

His lips moved over hers slowly, deliberately, as if he was savoring her. After only a few seconds she was clinging to him, his shirt fisted in her hands, her back arching as she tried to get closer.

Caitlyn felt his hand move to the back of her neck, holding her in place as he tasted her, his tongue sliding along her lower lip and then in against her tongue when she sighed.

When he finally lifted his head, she swore that she could still feel his tongue on hers. And in a few other places it hadn't actually been.

"Whoa," she breathed out.

He nodded. "Yeah."

"We should…"

"Stop."

"Do that again."

They spoke at the same time and stopped at the same time.

He let go of her and stepped back.

"You think we should stop," she said, trying not to show just how disappointed she was.

"You think we should keep going?" He looked a little stunned at that.

"I think I need another shot." She raised her hand and signaled the waitress.

She was definitely going to need another, because she'd just made a life-altering decision. Do or die. All or nothing. Play hard or go home.

Gulp.

CHAPTER SIX

Another shot was such a bad idea. But Eli tipped his head back, swallowing his third dose of Jäger anyway. The tryout was over. It was out of his hands. Nothing he could do. His life was currently in a strange limbo state between what he'd always known and what he'd always dreamed of. Tomorrow his life could change forever. Or not. But for tonight, he was floating between the two worlds.

It seemed appropriate somehow that he was floating with Caitlyn.

She was also something he'd always known and something he'd always dreamed of—even though he'd been pretty adamantly telling himself that he couldn't dream about her. He was no longer lying to himself. He wanted her. Good idea? No. Worst thing he'd ever done? Probably not. So, he was somewhere in between on that as well.

Caitlyn also took her third shot. The look on her face as she swallowed the liqueur was adorable.

"How many more shots do you need?" she asked.

He frowned. "What?"

"Well, it took two to get you to kiss me. You just had your third. I'm wondering how many you need to take me to bed."

He just stared at her. He blinked. He was pretty much raring to go right now, actually. "How many do *you* need?"

She gave him a smile that wasn't a bit tipsy. And was fully seductive. "I didn't need even one, Eli."

It was like his cock was voice-activated. All she'd done was *talk* and he was rock hard. "Damn, Cait."

"You can't be completely surprised."

Was he surprised? That she was attracted to him? That she wanted to sleep with him?

Yeah, he fucking was. Because if his mind had ever

even started to go in that direction, he would have shut it down.

"I don't need anything to want you," he said honestly.

"I'm going to need a few more to get me *past* that."

She took a long draw on her beer. After she swallowed, she nodded. "Okay, well, I'm going to need two more to get to drunk-enough-to-fall-asleep-even-knowing-you're-half-naked-in-the-next-bed and drunk-enough-to-not-even-get-up-in-the-night-for-the-bathroom."

Ah yes, the bathroom last night. As if that had been far from his mind all day.

"Two more it is," he agreed, even as his body screamed at him to shut the hell up.

If he kissed her again, if he kept going…well, from the look on Caitlyn's face, they both knew where that was going to lead them.

She ate a fry and took a drink of beer, then licked her lips clean of the salt.

An image of her on her knees, those lips and that tongue wetting some other things, flashed through his mind. He coughed and shook his head.

Then she raised her hand to the waitress again. She held up two fingers and waved them between her and Eli.

The girl brought four more shots over and set them in the middle of the table.

Caitlyn picked one up. "Okay, moment of truth. We drink these shots and we go to the hotel, to two separate beds, and home to Sapphire Falls tomorrow as friends. Or we don't take these shots and we go back to the hotel to *one* bed. And then go home to Sapphire Falls tomorrow as friends."

Damn, that second one sounded good. Too good to be true, actually.

He stared down at the shot glasses in front of him.

It would be so easy to just throw those back.

And it would be *so* easy not to.

Eli dragged in a deep breath and decided he needed to be honest. With them both.

"I want option two so badly I'm having trouble sitting here right now," he told her. "But you want to get married and have kids and grow old in Sapphire Falls." He paused, then said. "And I don't."

She frowned slightly.

"I mean, I might. That might be the way fate takes this thing. I don't know." He rubbed a hand over his chest that was suddenly feeling extremely tight. "But you made me realize, by dragging me down here, that I want this. I want more than I've had. I don't feel good about it all. I feel pretty fucking guilty." He swallowed and nodded, feeling some of the tightness around his heart loosen as he finally said this out loud. "I've been pushing what I want down deep because I do feel guilty wanting that when my family needs me. And I love my dad. And I resent what happened to him. And the store. And that I needed to come home. I resent Sapphire Falls sometimes. And…I don't want you to be something, or someone, I resent, Cait."

She was staring at him as she set the shot glass down with a thunk.

She slid off her stool and came around to stand in front of him. "I'm not going to let you give this up, Eli. Not for me or any reason. Neither will your dad. Or the town. As much as we all love you and love having you around, we also love you enough to want you to be happy. Why do you think we all forced you to come to the tryout? You might not believe in yourself but I believe enough for both of us."

She grabbed the front of his shirt and pulled him in. She put her lips to his and every thought but *all I want* evaporated from his brain.

It wasn't just the kiss. Though Caitlyn's lips were the sweetest he'd ever tasted, her sighs went straight to his cock and her ass seemed shaped specifically to fit in his hands, it wasn't just the kiss that fired his blood and made him need in a way he'd never needed before. It was her passion—for him. Not for him physically but for his dream. She believed in him. When he felt like he was chasing something meant for someone younger or fresher or less jaded or more advanced, she helped him see that he was talented and passionate and smart.

God, if he could just bottle that up. Just absorb all of the things Caitlyn Murray thought and felt for him and take it out anytime he needed a shot...

But maybe he could. He could have her in his life, couldn't he? Maybe it would be in little bits, maybe it would be over a long distance, but he knew, suddenly in that moment, that he needed her. He couldn't go to Kilby or San Diego or even back to Sapphire Falls tomorrow without having her in his system and in his life.

As he continued to kiss her, he dug for his wallet. He extracted some bills—he knew they were all twenties; it was all he'd been able to get out of the ATM—and threw them on the table. He lifted his head and stood, looking into her eyes. Without a word he picked up the shot glasses, crossed to the bar and put them down where two girls were sipping cocktails.

"Haven't been touched. Scout's honor," he told them.

Caitlyn's eyes widened at the message he'd just sent. No shots, one bed. That was the deal.

He came back to her and cupped her face in his hand, his thumb caressing the soft skin of her cheek. "Thank you."

"For kissing you?" She tipped her head and smiled impishly. "Anytime."

"In two minutes."

"What?"

"You said anytime. I'm going to need more in about two minutes."

"What's in two minutes?"

"We should be back to the hotel room by then."

CHAPTER SEVEN

Caitlyn's heart leapt to her throat as Eli grabbed her hand and started for the door.

He'd given away those last four shots. Was it crazy to see that as a pretty romantic gesture?

She was even able to keep up with his long strides as he headed across the parking lot and up the block to their hotel.

Neither of them said a word as he shoved the key card into the slot and then pushed the door open so hard it banged against the wall behind it. He reached for her and pulled her into the room with him. Then even better, he put his hands under her ass and lifted her so she had to wrap her legs around his waist. He kicked the door shut and put her up against it.

"You're sure about this?" he asked, putting his lips just behind her ear.

"God, yes," she assured him, her fingers digging into his shoulders. "Please."

He kissed behind her ear, then down the side of her neck. Goose bumps erupted over her entire body and her thighs tightened around him.

She had never wanted anything more. Even knowing he was leaving. Even knowing he *wanted* to leave. She wanted one night. If that's all she could have, she'd take it. And knowing it was only the one night would still keep her heart intact. This wasn't about forever, this wasn't about spend-our-lives-together love, this was...friendship gone wild.

She was good with that.

Caitlyn stroked her hands over his wide shoulders and down his back, touching all the places she'd been itching to for so long. His muscles bunched as he also ran his hands over her. The door behind her supported most of her weight and he was able to slide his big palms over her butt, the backs of her thighs and up her back to her head, where he threaded his fingers into her hair as he consumed her mouth again.

The kiss was filled with lust and sweetness at the same time. His tongue stroked boldly over her lip and she opened, showing him she was willing to give him anything he wanted. Their tongued tangled, their hands roamed, and the room filled with the sounds of need and pleasure.

Finally, he ripped his mouth from hers and, panting, stared into her eyes. "Need you naked. Now."

She nodded, unable to speak. He let her slide down the door, stepping back when her feet touched the floor. He yanked his t-shirt over his head, throwing it to the side.

Caitlyn drank in the sight—the golden skin, the contours of his muscles, the way his abs bunched as he undid his fly and shoved his jeans down while toeing off his shoes. Soon there was a pile of cotton and denim on top of his shoes and he was reaching for her again.

He left his boxers on but she could see the straining length of his erection and her palms literally tingled with the idea of finally touching him.

He slid her t-shirt up and over her head, pausing to admire her in only her bra and jeans.

"So pretty," he praised huskily, running the pad of his finger over the top edge of her bra.

Her nipples beaded instantly and she reached behind her for the hooks. She didn't want anything, not even her favorite bra, between them. She wanted his hands on her.

"Touch me, Eli," she said softly, flinging her bra to the side with the rest of their clothes.

"Oh, Candy-girl, there's no way I'm *not* going to be touching you."

She took his hand and lifted it to her breast. "Now."

His eyes darkened as he cupped her, running the pad of his thumb over the stiff point. "Now and for a long time to come," he promised, lowering his head again and kissing her.

Caitlyn felt as if she was feverish. She really thought she'd produce steam if someone poured cool water on her right now. She let her head fall back and hoped the door would hold her up as Eli kissed his way down her throat, licked her collar bone and then continued down until he took her nipple in his mouth.

She gripped the back of his head and whimpered. That was all she was able to do.

As he licked, then sucked, she was vaguely aware that he'd unbuttoned and unzipped her jeans and was working them down over her hips.

She kicked her shoes off and reached to help him, making sure he took her panties with the jeans. They were pink silk to match her bra, but she thought they were both probably beyond caring about her lingerie coordination.

She felt him lift his head and somehow pried her eyes open.

What was she doing with her eyes shut? She wanted to see all of this. She wanted to use *every* one of her senses to the fullest.

Eli was staring at her, his fists clenched at his sides, his chest heaving.

Caitlyn wet her lips. "You okay, Hotshot?"

He lifted his head. "I'm…so fucking okay. I'm just not sure where to start."

She grinned, feeling lighter and happier and *hotter* than she could remember feeling in a very long time. "Well then how about *I* start?"

She leaned forward, hooked her thumbs in the waistband of his boxers and slid them down—over that magnificent ass, powerful thighs, toned calves and huge feet. Once she'd divested him of his underwear, she ran her hands over that same path but in reverse. When she got to where she'd started, she wrapped a hand around the hot, hard length of his cock.

A breath hissed out from between his teeth and he suddenly bent and scooped her up. He took the five long strides to the bed—her bed from the night before—and lowered her onto the mattress, following her down.

He wasted no time running his hands all over her body, kissing her lips, then sucking on a nipple, then licking his way down the center of her belly, swirling his tongue in her belly button and continuing lower.

She had to part her thighs to make room for his broad shoulders and when she did, he gave an approving growl.

"Let's see just how sweet you really are," he muttered. Then he lowered his head.

Caitlyn's head pressed back into the pillow, her neck arching, her hands gripping the comforter on either side of her. Eli licked long and deep, then sucked on her clit, bringing her to the edge of an amazing orgasm within seconds. But before she could go over the edge, he lifted his head. "Oh, no, not without me," he told her.

He climbed up the length of her body, kissing her deeply as his hand slid over her belly and between her legs. She moaned as he pressed a finger deep, making nerve endings she'd almost forgotten about jump to life. He added another finger, sliding in and out as she ran her hands up and down his back.

He rolled away slightly, reaching for something on the floor—a condom, she hoped—and she took advantage of the position to again take him in hand.

He groaned, his eyes sliding shut. "Damn you feel good," he said roughly.

He flexed his butt, thrusting into her fist, and Caitlyn felt her body temperature hike.

She wanted him in her mouth. She started to wiggle down the bed, but he rolled, pinning her.

"Can't take that this time," he said, clearly reading what she'd been intending. His eyes were hot and he was breathing hard.

Caitlyn loved that she could do that to him. But "this time" indicated there would be another time. And there wouldn't. Not past tonight anyway. Any next time for them had to be before the sun came up. She wanted everything with him—every position, every dirty word, every fantasy. They had a lot to do tonight.

"Hope you recover quickly," she said with a smile.

Something flickered in his gaze. "I have a feeling that recovering might not be possible."

Caitlyn's heart pounded against her rib cage. Damn. That was sweet. And made her hope it was true. And made her sad.

Why did she have to fall in love with a guy with dreams that would take him away? Dreams that would take him away, possibly, tomorrow? That call would come soon, she knew it.

She pulled him fully on top of her and wrapped her legs around his waist, his cock pressing hotly against her. "Come on, Hotshot, you know how to rally."

He reached between them, his knuckles brushing over her most sensitive flesh, as he rolled on the condom. The condom he'd, thank God, had close.

Then he braced himself on his elbows and looked down at her. "You're amazing," he said, repeating the words they'd said to one another a number of times already on this trip.

"Ditto," she whispered.

And they'd only made it to third base so far. Okay, maybe halfway to home.

She expected him to thrust into her, but he took it slow, easing in and pulling out again in long, deep, sweet, hot strokes.

Her breath caught. It was the most glorious physical experience of her life and…so much more.

Damn, he was right about the recovering thing. Wasn't

going to happen. Already.

He continued to move slow and easy, his words low and sweet, things like "so good", "like I dreamed", "can't believe it." But it only took a few minutes for the heat and emotion to build to a point where they needed an outlet.

"More, Eli," she breathed. "Harder. Faster."

He groaned and picked up the pace, and that was all it took for the heat and friction to combine into a delicious wave of pleasure.

Caitlyn moved with him, pressing against him, her own words tumbling from her lips—"yes" and "like that" and "more"—until she was climbing toward her climax.

"Come with me, Cait," he said against her ear. "I need to feel that. Don't hold back."

She couldn't have held back if she'd wanted to. "Eli—"

And then the orgasm was sweeping over her, waves of hot pleasure consuming her. She cried out and felt her body clamping onto his just as he groaned "Caitlyn" in a low, sexy growl that made the ripples of her orgasm go on and on.

Finally, the waves quieted and her limbs began to notice sensations other than tingles.

Caitlyn let her arms flop to her sides and Eli eased himself off of her, though he didn't go far.

He slung his arm over her stomach and pressed against her entire right side, hot and heavy and absolutely the best thing she'd ever felt.

She got her mouth on him finally too. Twice.

Caitlyn thought back over the night as she drove them back to Sapphire Falls the next day. Eli snored softly in the passenger seat, but he'd twined his fingers with hers and their hands rested on the center console between them.

She was happy.

Too happy.

It was going to end. Today probably. Tonight. Tomorrow. Soon. The official call would only come if the Friars wanted Eli, but Stewart, the scout, had promised to call no matter what. To her mind, that was a great sign. Why would he say something like that if Eli didn't have a good shot? Besides, she'd done a little online research and she knew that the Friars were looking for good pitching. Caleb Hart was their star—and he was amazing—but Yazmer Perez had melted down as soon as he hit the major leagues. They *needed* someone like Eli Anderson.

She had no doubts whatsoever. Eli would be leaving soon.

But she also had no regrets. Not about last night. Or early this morning. Or later this morning.

She was still grinning when she pulled up in front of his house.

He leaned over to kiss her and said softly, "Want to see you tonight."

She wanted to see him too. But now things could get dangerous. Seeing him in Sapphire Falls would feel more…real. It would feel more like what she wanted long term. It would give her more to miss.

"How about you come over and tell me when you get the call from Stewart?"

He frowned slightly. "It might not be today."

She put her hand against his cheek. "It will be today."

He looked a little sad as he took her hand and kissed the palm. "Maybe."

"What's wrong?"

"I'm not sure how I want that call to go."

Her heart flipped even as she gave him a stern look. "Yes you do. Stop it. Come over after you hear."

"It might be a no."

"It won't be a no."

"It could be."

"Eli." She sighed. "I'll *bet* you that it's a yes."

His face brightened a little at that. "What do I get if I win?"

She smiled. "If it's a no, you get whatever you want from me. And if it's a yes," her heart squeezed at that but she went on, "I get whatever I want from you."

He grinned and kissed her again. "Deal."

She watched him walk up to his front door and felt a strange combination of happiness, sadness, hope and dread.

Caitlyn was unpacked an hour later and trying to *not* go over and over—and over and over—last night in her mind.

But it had been so…

And he was so…

And now she was so…

The doorbell rang and she almost wept with relief. A distraction. She'd been this close to calling Bryan to offer to do the bar inventory.

She pulled the door open with a huge smile for whoever was saving her from her lusty daydreams.

Funny thing, the subject of those lusty daydreams was standing with an arm propped on her doorframe.

"Eli. Hi."

"I got the call."

Her heart flipped, her stomach swirled and her mind spun. She swallowed hard. "And?"

"You won the bet."

"I won the bet." With her mind so flustered, it took her a moment to understand what that meant. "*You got the call?*"

"I got the call. I'm in. I report to the Kilby Catfish tomorrow." A huge grin split his face, while her heart splintered into a million conflicting pieces.

He's amazing. He deserves this. He's leaving. It hurts. So much. But don't let him see it.

"Oh my God, Eli! You did it! You got the call!" she shrieked and gave a little jump, maybe going a wee bit overboard to hide the hole opening in her heart.

"And you won the bet. You know what that means." He lowered his voice. "I'm here to give you whatever you want." He stepped inside, filling her world with his hard muscles and smoldering blue eyes. Her body responded with a helpless throb, while her heart wanted to shrivel up and disappear.

The thing was—what she wanted was the one thing he couldn't give her.

Him.

CHAPTER EIGHT

In the home dugout at Catfish Stadium, Eli sat with the other rookies watching slugger Trevor Stark toy with a young Aces pitcher. The poor dude was so red in the face, he looked as if he was being roasted over a barbecue pit. Not only was it hot as hell in Texas in July, but pitching to the powerhouse Stark would make an All-Star sweat.

"When are the Friars going to call that guy up?" Eli asked Dwight Conner, the center fielder, who was casually working his way through a package of sunflower seeds.

"Million-dollar question. He keeps messing up whenever he gets close. I love the guy like a brother, but even I don't know why he keeps screwing up his shot. It's almost like he does it on purpose. Tell you what, though. When he leaves Kilby, half the girls here will go into mourning."

Okay then. Eli still wasn't used to the attention ballplayers got in Kilby—and not just the stars like Trevor Stark. The first time a kid had asked him to sign a baseball, he'd fumbled the pen and dropped the ball in a storm drain. Not too embarrassing.

"What about you, Nebraska? You got a girl back home?"

"Bet he doesn't," said Ramirez, the tough-looking, tattooed third baseman. "He's got that married look. Like me."

"Married look?" Jim Lieberman, the shortstop everyone called "Bieberman" because he looked just like Justin Bieber, eyed Eli with fascination. "What makes you say that?"

"Watch him the next time he pitches. Comes off the mound, goes right into the dugout. Do not pass go, do not play eye-footsie with the ladies."

"I do the same thing, and I'm not married."

"That's different, Beeb. That's because you can't see over the top of the dugout," Dwight needled him with a grin.

Bieberman glared at him, but in a good-natured way; clearly he was used to the teasing. "A round of drinks at the Roadhouse says Eli's not married."

"Done."

"Eli?"

"Not married."

"You're buying, Dwight." Jim Lieberman started to give Eli a high-five, but Dwight held up one big hand.

"Hang on. Mr. Anderson," Dwight made his voice sound like the character from the *Matrix*, "if that girl up there," Dwight pointed to a gorgeous redhead in the stands, "offered to get naked with you, what would you say to her?"

The other guys hooted loudly enough to make Trevor shoot a glare from the batter's box.

Eli's face heated up. "I'd...uh...pass."

"You'd pass because..." Dwight leaned closer, eyebrows raised expectantly.

"Because..." How the hell could he explain this? He'd left things so unsettled with Caitlyn. All that hot sex was imprinted on his brain, body and soul, right next to a lifetime's worth of friendship. He didn't know where things stood with Caitlyn, but he did know one thing for sure. The redhead didn't interest him. Nor did the hot blonde next to her, or the Beyoncé lookalike in the next row. And that was because... "Okay, fine, there's a girl. Back home. But it's just casual. We're not married."

Now it was Ramirez and Dwight's turn to high-five. "Not married *yet*," Ramirez said in triumph. "You've got the married look. No hiding it. First round's on the Beeb."

"But...but...he said he's not..." While Bieberman sputtered in protest, Trevor hit a slamming line drive right through the gap between first and second.

Eli jumped to his feet and cheered with the rest of the guys. *Saved by a line drive.*

He'd been a Kilby Catfish for exactly one week, two days, and three hours, and he'd spent approximately two thirds of that time thinking about Caitlyn Murray. She would have filled even more of his thoughts if their one incredible night hadn't happened right before he got the call. But adjusting to a completely different existence took up a lot of his attention.

He was a professional ballplayer now. It was really true. There was a locker in the clubhouse marked by a strip of masking tape with the name Eli Anderson and the number 29. He was a *professional ballplayer*. Every time he walked into the clubhouse, he expected someone—the intimidating Trevor Stark, maybe—to tell him to get the hell out.

Not that everyone hadn't been welcoming. The wild and crazy Catfish had greeted him just like any other new arrival.

With pranks.

During his first bullpen session, every single one of his pitches had fallen exactly six inches short. He'd been sweating like a pig, trying to get that extra distance, when Dwight Conner happened by.

"Hey, Nebraska, you always move the rubber back half a foot when you work out?"

The other pitchers had cracked up and Eli had turned beet red, then moved the rubber back to its proper location.

He didn't mind that prank. He didn't mind the teasing. He didn't mind the relentless critiques from Mitch the pitching coach, or being brought in for one inning of work at the end of a losing game, or warming up only to sit on his ass in the dugout.

He loved it all. Every grass-scented, sweaty, muscle-straining moment.

Only one thing was missing. If only Caitlyn could be

here. He longed for her with an intensity that kind of shocked him, to be honest. He wanted to share this amazing experience with her. He wanted to see her in the stands, go home to her at night. Instead, he was sharing a mostly unfurnished apartment with two other players.

The place smelled like sweaty socks and Chinese food. And he lay there every night trying to bury all those sensual memories from Kansas City.

He was a jackass, straight-up. Caitlyn had made it totally clear that their hookup was a one-time thing. When he'd rushed over to her house to tell her he got the call, he'd assumed they'd celebrate in bed. Naked. All night long, and maybe until his plane left.

Instead Caitlyn had celebrated by calling everyone in Sapphire Falls to share the news. Then she'd made homemade Cracker Jacks for the entire town. He hadn't gotten a single second alone with her between then and the moment when he'd stepped on that plane.

Obviously, Caitlyn wanted to put Kansas City behind them. Which made sense. They wanted different things; they were headed in different directions. Casual, that's what things were between them.

Casual.

He could do casual. He'd done it before. He'd walked away from several beautiful women because his responsibilities to his family and the business took all his time. He knew that drill down cold.

So why couldn't he do the same thing with Caitlyn Murray? Maybe because she was the sweetest, sexiest, kindest, sassiest girl he'd ever known?

Thanks to Trevor's three-run homer in the eighth inning, the game ended in a win for the Catfish, which put everyone in a good mood. The clubhouse quickly filled with ballplayers in various stages of nakedness. A reporter snagged Trevor to talk about his game-winning homer, while the other players talked trash and joked around. Eli still felt like an outsider, so he skipped the post-game chatter and headed straight for the shower.

Which made him think about the shower he and Caitlyn had taken together in Kansas City before hitting the road. The one in which he'd soaped every inch of her body, then licked her sweet, plump little clit until she came over and over, her moans echoing off the tiles of the shower stall.

How had he never realized what a sex goddess Caitlyn was?

He braced his hand on the tile, letting the water stream down his body. Caitlyn might want to *pretend* things were casual, but she couldn't hide her reactions to him. And yeah, they might be a thousand miles apart, but technology was his friend.

Back in the locker room, he dried off, tied a towel around his hips, then dug through his gear for his phone. He'd noticed the way she looked at his bare chest; it was almost as lustful as the way he ate up every curve of her delicious body. He snapped a shot of himself and fired it off in a text, along with the words, *Live from Kilby, Texas.*

After a moment, she answered. *You did NOT just send me a locker-room selfie.*

He grinned, imagining her sassy eye-roll. *It's like a postcard without the stamp.*

So true. OMG, who's that gorgeous hunk in the background?

What? He pulled up the photo and peered at it. Oh damn. He'd managed to get a piece of Trevor Stark's chiseled rear-end in the shot.

Delete. DELETE.

Sure. After I blow it up to poster size and hang it on my bedroom wall.

That's not the ass that belongs in your bedroom.

ROFLMAO. Did you just call yourself an ass?

Crap. Maybe technology wasn't his friend after all. He ran his hand through his still-damp hair, trying to figure out a way to salvage this conversation.

Passing by, Ramirez snapped a towel at him. "Married look."

"Not married," Eli said through gritted teeth.

"Uh-huh."

Irritated, Eli addressed the entire clubhouse of half-dressed players. He needed to make a statement, right here, right now, for his own sake as much as anyone else's. "Anyone up for the Roadhouse tonight? *Single* guy looking to have some fun here."

"Awwright. Time to initiate the rookie!" Dwight called above the chorus of "yups" and "hell yeahs."

The Kilby Roadhouse was the favorite hangout of the Catfish and half the town of Kilby. It was a fun spot, a big open space with worn wooden floor planks and red chili pepper lights strung along the walls. Its homey feel reminded Eli of the Come Again. Which, of course, reminded him of Caitlyn. He ate a burger and a beer, talked a little baseball with the bartender and a few players. But when he found himself ordering a shot of Jäger and telling Dwight about how Caitlyn had kidnapped him and taken him to the tryout, he threw in the towel. As Ramirez cackled and clapped him on the back, he grabbed his jacket and headed for the exit.

"Married look," Ramirez mouthed over a country beat he didn't recognize.

Whatever. If he had the "married look," it was thanks to all his responsibilities, not his confusing, all-over-the-place feelings for Caitlyn. Right?

On his way out, he nearly bumped into Trevor Stark, whose icy-blond good looks and the scar on his cheek gave him the air of a Viking conqueror. Every girl in the place seemed to be craning her neck to catch his eye. Casual in jeans and a dark gray t-shirt, Trevor shrugged off the attention and nodded to Eli.

"Good game," Eli said, still intimidated by the man.

Trevor paused just inside the door. "You're the new pitcher from Nebraska, right?"

"Yeah." Eli was honestly a little surprised Trevor recognized him.

"That's a crazy-ass knuckleball you got. Glad I don't have to hit it."

For a moment, Eli thought the star was mocking him. "Well, they outlawed the spitball, so knuckleball it is."

But Trevor didn't laugh the way he would have if his compliment had been a joke. Instead, he studied Eli for a long moment. "You got something special there, Nebraska. But it's not worth much if you don't believe in it."

Eli's jaw practically dropped. Was Stark giving him advice?

He flashed on something Caitlyn had said. *You might not believe in yourself but I believe enough for both of us.*

A girl's gushing voice interrupted. "Trevor, oh my God, that home run was *amaaazing!*"

Trevor turned to greet her, the scar on his cheek catching Eli's eye. Where had that come from? The left fielder sure was a man of mystery. And he'd taken the time to offer Eli advice. That realization flooded him with something he couldn't quite name. A sense of...belonging, he supposed.

With a last nod of goodbye, he left Trevor to his fans and exited the Roadhouse.

When he reached the parking lot, which was just starting to fill up with pickups and motorcycles, he pulled out his phone. Just in case any important messages had come in, not because of Cait...

Adrenaline surged in his veins when he saw that Caitlyn had, in fact, sent a text.

Things just aren't the same here without you.

She'd attached a photo from the hardware store. Jimmy the stock boy posed with a plunger latched onto his cheek, his eyes rolling up into his head. Goofing off for Caitlyn, that's what he was doing. Eli could practically hear their laughter.

A crazy pang of jealousy lodged in his gut. Which was insane. A Triple-A pitcher feeling jealous of a hardware store stock boy? What was wrong with him? Would he really rather be back in Sapphire Falls than Kilby? Of course not—he was living his dream. Well, sort of, one late-relief inning at a time.

That was the real problem. Duke, the manager, still hadn't tapped him to start a game. He was trying him out, watching how he worked. Eli wasn't living his dream *yet*. That wouldn't happen until his name was in the lineup as the starting pitcher.

When that happened, *then* maybe he'd be able to chase away all these thoughts of home. Of Caitlyn. Not that they were the same. Or were they?

୨~ଙ୬

At Scott's Sweets Shop, Caitlyn was arranging a new batch of white-chocolate-covered strawberries in the display case when Tim Watkins' face appeared on the other side of the glass. She jumped, bumping her head on the edge. With one hand massaging the tender spot, she rose to her feet.

"What are you doing here, Tim?"

"Just wondering what you're doing tonight. My date cancelled on me. Want to go to the movies? I got tickets for *Jackass 7*."

"Wow, with an invitation like that, what girl could resist?"

Tim stared at her blankly, pushing his baseball cap so the bill pointed backwards. "What do you mean? I said I got tickets. That means I'm paying."

Ugh, Tim was so clueless. Why did *he* have to have an undying crush on her, and not a certain other baseball-cap-wearing guy? Come to think of it, why did Tim have to wear a baseball cap at all? It just made her think about Eli. Not that she wasn't already thinking about him. Much.

Her cellphone pinged, which gave her a bright starburst of anticipation. Maybe it was a text from Eli. "I'm working tonight, Tim. Sorry."

He didn't move. Her cell phone was burning a hole in her pocket, crying out to her. *Check me, check me!* "Do you mind? I have to take this."

"I'm kind of, like, a customer, Cait. Don't you have to serve me?"

She gritted her teeth together. "Fine. What do you kind of, like, want?"

He tilted his head, pretending to ponder the options displayed in the bakery case. "I've heard good things about the mini-cheesecakes."

"Yeah, they're one of our biggest sellers."

He bent to scan the case. "Those gingerbread kittens are suh-weet."

"Yup." Her cell dinged again. *Check me, check me!* Maybe she could angle it in her pocket so she could read through the thin cotton of her sundress. Tim would never notice. He'd think she was checking out her own boobs or something, because that's how his caveman mind worked.

"Do you have anything gluten-free?" he was asking.

Caitlyn was afraid her head might explode. "Tim. If you don't make up your mind in two seconds, you're getting stale fruitcake from last Christmas."

"Touchy, touchy. Fine, go ahead and check your phone. Must be important. I'll wait."

Whistling innocently, he ambled through the store while she pulled out her phone and devoured the message as if it was a mini-cheesecake with extra strawberries.

Dreamed about you last night. You were wearing those cupcake pajamas. I licked the sleeve and it turned out they were made of pink frosting. Turns out I REALLY like pink frosting. A smiley face with a tongue sticking out came next.

Caitlyn's face burned as the image of Eli licking pink frosting off her body took over her imagination. He would be naked, of course, that sexy bare chest braced over her, muscles flexed as he ran his tongue over her nipple, swirling it around to lap up every last particle of the sweet temptation—

"How's Eli?"

"Amazing," she answered automatically, her gaze shooting up to find Tim peering over the glass case in front of her. "I mean, he's doing amazing down in Texas."

She nervously brushed a strand of hair away from her face. Big mistake, because in the process she fumbled her phone, which spurted out of her hand and skidded across the top of the glass case. *Crap.* If Tim saw that last message, the entire town would know she and Eli were text-flirting. She slammed her hand over the phone so fast Tim jumped.

With her phone safely cradled against her chest, she backed away from the display case. That's when her butt bumped against a tray of maple syrup candies cooling on the counter. She spun around in time to see the tray tilt over the edge and a few candies rain to the floor.

If Tim didn't leave soon, the place would be a wreck.

"Get out," she ordered him.

"Fine. But you can't sell those anymore, right?" Tim asked hopefully, eyeing the candy on the floor.

"Out."

"Okay, okay. Say hi to Eli for me." He smirked. "You and Eli. Never would have thought, after what happened on New Year's."

She wished she'd never kissed Tim at all. The only good thing about kissing him was that now she had something to compare the real thing with. No kiss had ever felt as good as Eli's.

On impulse, she picked up one of the maple syrup candies and flung it after him. "On the house," she called.

He spun around and caught it against his chest. "Nice arm. Learn that from your *boyfriend*?"

The door clanged shut behind him. She puffed out a breath and knelt to pick up the rest of the fallen candies. *Fan*tastic. Obviously, Tim knew something was going on between her and Eli. She had no idea *how* he knew. Bryan? Ty? The bartender at *Eddie's*? Even worse, if Tim knew that meant everyone in Sapphire Falls knew that she and Eli were...whatever they were. Superhot sex buddies? Friends with benefits so good they ought to be illegal?

Come to think of it, that explained all the traffic Scott's Sweets had experienced over the last few days. People were curious, or maybe nosy was a better word. The candy shop had been ridiculously busy lately, to the extent she was starting to worry about the combined blood sugar level of Sapphire Falls.

Could gossip lead to hyperglycemia? At this rate, she wouldn't be surprised.

She looked back at Eli's text. *Pink frosting.* Hmmm.

Smiling, she texted him back. *Speaking of frosting, your birthday's coming up.* If she was remembering right—and she wouldn't forget, because birthdays were her favorite holidays—his was in two days.

It took only a moment for him to answer back. *You know what I want for my birthday.*

A perfect game?

A perfect girl. In my bed. In her birthday suit.

Chills danced down her spine. *A perfect girl.* Did he mean *her*? Did that mean he thought of her as more than just the "friend" he'd slept with right before leaving town?

When he'd gotten on that plane to Houston, she'd assumed that would be it for them. She'd get updates from Chip, or from Bryan. Maybe read about him in the paper or see him pitch on TV. He was headed into the big wide world, where baseball groupies would be asking for his autograph on their body parts. While she was still back in Sapphire Falls, fending off Tim Watkins.

In my bed, Eli had texted. There was literally no place on earth she'd rather be. It didn't matter where the bed was. Sapphire Falls, Kilby, San Diego, where his bed was, she wanted to be in it.

But she couldn't leave Bryan, so this wasn't going to go anywhere, so why torture herself? If she was smart, she'd let him go right now. She'd stop texting, stop dreaming, stop remembering.

Might as well ask her to stop transforming oxygen into carbon dioxide. Loving Eli was like some basic chemical reality of her existence. It wasn't going to change.

Ack!! She stuck a maple candy in her mouth and let the sweetness melt into her tongue. She needed to take her mind off this dead-end also known as the "hottest night of her life" and "the guy she'd never get over." Her life was here in Sapphire Falls, and she needed to accept that.

On impulse, she picked up the phone and called Hailey, who used to be the mayor.

"This is Caitlyn. I'd like to volunteer," she said as soon as Hailey answered.

"Volunteer for what?" She sounded sleepy—probably from cuddling all night with her own hot athlete, Ty.

"Anything. Everything. Sign me up. Tell me who to call. I'll organize the next festival. What is it? Fourth of July? Bastille Day? Founder's Day? I don't even care. What else is going on? Any big charity projects that need an extra hand?"

"Are you okay, honey?"

"I'm on top of the world. Seriously." She rearranged the gingerbread kittens into cute little paired couples. "I've got a lot to offer, Hailey."

"Of course you do."

"And I'm offering it all to Sapphire Falls."

A long pause, while Hailey whispered something to someone. Caitlyn winced. She was probably telling Ty that Bryan's little sister had just gone off the deep end. "Let me get back to you, okay?"

"Sure thing. Thanks. But I'm serious, Hailey!"

"Just hang on. I'll figure something out."

Caitlyn hung up, and saw that a few more texts from Eli had come in while she'd been talking. She squeezed her eyes shut. *Don't look. Move on with your life.*

Yeah, right. Like that was going to happen. Like she hadn't stared at the photo Eli had sent from the locker room for two hours straight.

She opened one eye and read his text. *Just got the word. Duke finally scheduled me to start. Friday, baby! My first start as a pro ballplayer. Can you believe it?*

Of course she could believe it. She believed in Eli to the bottom of her soul. He was destined for something great.

She sent back a stream of emoticons, including a confetti hat, a bottle of champagne, an excited smiley face, and a baseball bat.

And then it hit her. *Friday.*

Friday was Eli's birthday.

CHAPTER NINE

The next day, Ty showed up at the Murray house. He bounded into the kitchen, where they were all having breakfast. He had an overnight bag slung over one shoulder and a huge grin on his face.

"Bryan and Caitlyn, get your butts in the car. We're going on a road trip."

"What?" Her spoon halfway to her mouth, Caitlyn stared at the Olympic star. Even for Ty, this was unusual.

"I'm ready," said Bryan, setting down his bowl. "My bag's packed. So is Caitlyn's."

"*What?*" Caitlyn was sure everyone had lost their minds. "I haven't packed anything."

"I did it." Bryan smiled smugly. "You never even noticed, did you? I'm telling you, I could be a secret agent in this wheelchair. My stealth is unbelievable. Bags are in my room, Ty."

"Hang on here. What is going on? What road trip are you crazy people talking about? I can't go on a road trip. I have work. And...stuff to do."

"It's all arranged." Ty grinned. "I got you the time off, no problem. You have about a year of vacation coming. And Hailey said she'd really appreciate it if I took you off her hands for a while. Finding volunteer opportunities for you is kind of a time-suck."

"But..." She looked helplessly at her mother, who looked just as confused. "Bryan..."

"Will be with us. I cleared it with his doctor and the PT Nazi. They said a change of scene would be good."

In fact, Bryan looked more revved up than she'd seen him in a while. "I'm not missing another road trip. I have to get used to that wheelchair, and this is a good reason to try."

"Honey, you know the wheelchair is just temporary,"

their mother murmured. Caitlyn and Bryan exchanged a look. Why couldn't she accept the situation for what it was? She wanted things to be back to normal, and didn't understand that they never would be.

"I'm still totally confused," Caitlyn told the two guys. "Where is this road trip to?"

"Do you really think we'd let our boy Eli pitch his first professional start *on his birthday* without some hometown support? Is that how we do it in Sapphire Falls? I don't think so. Where is your brain? Never mind, don't answer that. I don't want to know." Ty flipped her hair, and she barely noticed because she was so shocked.

"You mean..."

"I mean we're going to Kilby, Texas."

"*What?* I can't go to Kilby. I'm not going. You guys can go."

Bryan rolled his chair so he was blocking her against the breakfast bar. "You'd let me travel all alone with that maniac? I need you."

"Besides," added Ty, moving next to Bryan. "No one does birthdays like Caitlyn Murray."

"That's true," she admitted, not boasting, but because it was the simple truth.

Everyone knew that birthdays were her thing. Who could forget the adorable Little Mermaid cupcakes she'd made for Annie Golden's sixth birthday. And the "75 and Still Hot to Trot" pony-shaped cake she'd made for Mrs. Burns at Sapphire Ranch.

Birthdays were important, even to pro ballplayers. Celebrating the day a person was born, letting that person know how glad you were they were part of your life, she loved all that.

Suddenly ideas were flitting through her brain...sweet, naughty, inspired ideas. "Fine, I'll come on the road trip with you guys. But we have to make a couple of stops first. I need to pick something up at Scott's Sweets. And it has to be a surprise. No one can tell Eli we're coming. This is going to be the best birthday he ever had."

Ty and Bryan whooped and exchanged high-fives.

"Done," said Bryan. "I'll meet you guys at the van."

Caitlyn went with Ty to pick up their bags from Bryan's bedroom. She fully intended to add a few items. If she was going to see Eli on his birthday, she was going to do it right.

"You know, Caitlyn, it's a good thing you agreed to come with us," Ty told her as they crossed the living room.

"Why?"

"Otherwise, we were going to kidnap you."

ఞ౿

Eli had never been so nervous in his life. He'd always been completely cool and confident before a start, all through Little League, varsity, and his one year of college ball. Okay, so he'd maybe gotten a few jitters during his first start at the U of N, but nothing like this. He paced around the dugout while a third-grader from the Kilby Baptist Church belted out the "Star-Spangled Banner".

As she finished, the crowd cheered and waved the Catfish-blue cowboy hats that had been handed out at the gates. It was Cowboy Appreciation Night at the stadium. Everyone wearing cowboy boots got a free hot dog, a massive line-dance had taken over the field before the anthem was sung, and Crush Taylor, the owner, had vowed to ride a mechanical bull on the field during the seventh-inning stretch.

That was the minor leagues for you. Every game had a promotion going on, the wackier the better.

Eli tried to block it all out and focus on his pitching strategy. Mike Solo, the Friars' talented reserve catcher, was back in Triple-A rehabbing from a strained thumb. The Catfish players kept teasing him that he'd gotten the injury

on purpose to spend time with his fiancée, Donna
MacIntyre, the promotions girl. Solo was only down for a
few days, but Eli had taken advantage by picking his brain
at every opportunity. The fact that Solo would be catching
his first start was the best birthday gift he could have
gotten.

Not that he'd told anyone it was his birthday. He was
here to pitch and help the team, not play birthday boy.

Solo came up next to him and clapped him on the
shoulder. "How're you feeling, big guy?"

"Awesome," said Eli weakly.

"If awesome is code for 'want to throw up,' I believe
you." The curly-haired catcher winked one green eye. "You
got this, Nebraska." Apparently that was his new nickname
all around. "You got it in the bag."

"You think?"

"Yeah, I do. Think of it this way. It can't be worse than
Caleb Hart's first game as a Catfish. I think they actually
put it in the record books under 'Suckiest Starts of All
Time.'"

"That right?" Eli worked at the leather of his glove,
wondering how that applied to him. Caleb Hart was a rising
star on the Friars. He'd even won the Cy Young Award the
year before. But he was a flame-thrower, unlike Eli, who
relied on finesse and that sneaky knuckleball.

"Hey." Mike Solo seemed to sense where his thoughts
were headed. "Forget Hart. This is about you. You got the
stuff, man. Just be yourself out there. And you got a secret
weapon, too."

"What's that?"

"Me." Mike grinned. "I know all those Isotopes hitters
better than my old Little League team. We got this." He
clapped him on the shoulder again. For an embarrassing
moment, Eli wanted to hug him. Mike Solo was a good
guy, straight up.

The young singer turned in a circle, as if overwhelmed

by the applause. Donna ran onto the field and, smiling kindly at the girl, took her hand to lead her in the right direction.

"That's my girl," said Mike softly, beaming with love and pride as he watched Donna.

Eli felt a surge of envy. What would it be like to have your favorite girl in the world, your *fiancée*, by your side during a game? To be able to soak in her smile, draw strength from her presence? Know you weren't ever alone?

He couldn't think about that now. He had to focus on the game and the parade of Isotopes batters who wanted to bash the stuffing out of him.

As the crowd applauded, the Catfish ran onto the field to take their positions. Eli jogged to the mound. It seemed enormous. And it was in the middle of *everything.* The entire diamond, the entire freaking *stadium* was built around that pile of dirt where he now stood. All those people were looking at him. Waiting for him. And they weren't asking where to find the drywall screws, or what brand of polyurethane to buy.

No, they were waiting *to see him pitch.* Holy hell.

Mike Solo squatted behind home plate and gestured for him to take his first warmup pitch. On autopilot, he reared back and let fly a damn good fastball. He heard a few claps from the stands, an approving "that's the way" from Mike—

Then a very familiar "yeah, baby!" from the box seat along the third base line.

He whirled toward the box, snagging the ball back from Solo as he turned.

Sure enough, there was Bryan. And Ty. And…her face as bright as sunshine… Caitlyn.

જ∞◅ુ

Did Eli have to be so unbearably sexy in his Catfish

uniform? Caitlyn couldn't tear her eyes from his strong
form as he took the mound. The fact that they'd been naked
in bed together…that he'd had his hands all over her
body…that she'd put her lips on his…

Oh God, don't think about that now! She felt a little
faint with the Texas sun beating down on their heads. She
raised her hand to shield her eyes, and that's when she saw
the exact moment he caught sight of their little group.

He straightened in shock, then let fly a huge grin. Did
those blue eyes linger on her, or was that her imagination?
He looked happy to see all of them. "Happy birthday,
dude!" Ty yelled. Eli tipped his cap to the three of them,
then turned back to the catcher, who was standing behind
the plate, his mask up, squinting back and forth between Eli
and the Sapphire Falls group.

"Play ball," called the umpire.

Right. There was a ball game to be played. Caitlyn sank
into her seat and tried to calm her racing heartbeat.

Eli looked *so good*. He'd always looked good to her,
even at the end of a long day at the hardware store,
frowning over cash register receipts. But now, there was
the way his uniform molded to his muscular legs. And then
there was the focused look on his face as he leaned in for
the sign from the catcher. And what about the way his
broad shoulders strained his jersey. And the way his brown
hair curled a bit under the back of his cap. The air of
confidence he exuded on the mound—not arrogance, not
cockiness, just… Rightness.

Quiet command, that was Eli. That was how he dealt
with Chip's doctors, Lindsay's teachers, and the staff at the
hardware store. Eli wasn't about boasting and bluster.

He was about getting the job done.

On the field and in more…intimate situations.

Her face flamed at the memory of what had happened
in that hotel room. Face it. The massive crush she'd been
working on in Sapphire Falls was nothing compared to this

feeling. She'd taken him inside her body. He'd taken her to levels of bliss that had blown her mind. And now she was watching him do his thing on the mound at a real baseball stadium.

How was she ever supposed to get over him?

Chewing on her bottom lip, she glanced over at Ty to see him watching her with amusement. "Everything okay there, Cait?"

Oh God. Did he know the sort of thoughts that were cruising around her brain right now? She fixed her gaze on Eli as he slid a curveball past a swinging Isotopes player.

"Strike three!" Bryan yelled. "Yeah, baby. Go, Eli!"

A smile quirked the corner of Eli's mouth, but otherwise he ignored the crowds in the stands. He accepted the ball back from the catcher, then watched the next batter step into the box.

Caitlyn leaned closer to her brother. "He really knows what he's doing, doesn't he?"

"Looks that way to me. I think the locals agree." He pointed to a sign in the stands behind home plate.

A curvy girl in blue jeans and a cowboy hat held up a homemade sign that read, "Just call me Mrs. Anderson."

A hot stab of jealousy hit her right in the stomach. *Mrs. Anderson?* Puh-lease. Totally tacky. She would never do such a thing. Why, she ought to run over there and tear that sign right out of her hands. Maybe take a lighter to it while she was at it. And stomp that blue cowboy hat to pieces.

"Whoa there, cowgirl," said Bryan, putting a hand on her arm. "Let's not get into any trouble with the hometown crowd. This is Texas. I think they hand out guns at the border."

"I'm...not..." She realized she was on her feet, glaring across the diamond. "I just think it's inappropriate, that's all. She doesn't even know Eli."

"She's a fan," said Ty. "She likes his pitching. You know you've hit the big time when you have groupies." He smiled smugly.

Ty ought to know about groupies, that was for sure. But Ty was... Ty. He'd always been a little wild, sort of a player. Eli wasn't like that. He was steady, responsible, the kind of guy you could always count on, who...who...looked like a freaking god in those baseball pants.

She sank back into her seat as Eli began pitching to the next batter. Calm and unflappable, he worked the outside corner with a fastball-curve-knuckleball sequence that had the batter grounding out to first base. From someone's portable TV, an announcer's voice accompanied the action.

"Other than a few innings spent mopping up other pitchers' messes, this is the first chance we've had to see Eli Anderson in action. What's your take so far, Bob?"

"Well, he ain't flashy, that's for sure. But you can see him thinking out there, taking his time with each pitch. That's rare for a rookie and shows a kind of maturity that will serve him well. If I had to sum up his play in one word, it might be intelligent."

"Good choice. I have to say I agree. But then every once in a while he delivers one of those wacky knuckleballs, and what can you say to that? They go about sixty miles an hour, but there's no way to predict a pitch like that. Word has it the Friars picked him for that pitch alone. It sure sets him apart from the crowd. The question now is, will the knuckleball make a comeback?"

Caitlyn glowed with pride. "I can't believe they're talking about Eli on the radio! And I knew the knuckleball wasn't a mistake. He was so worried about that."

Bryan gave her a funny smile. "You know something, Cait?"

"What?"

"I hope Eli knows how lucky he is."

The look on her brother's face—almost sad, as if he was saying goodbye to something—caught her off guard.

"Of course he knows. He never thought he'd have the chance to pitch professionally."

"That's not what I meant, and you know it."

Embarrassed, Caitlyn looked away from her brother. If he was talking about her and Eli, he was jumping to some crazy conclusions. Just then she caught sight of Stewart, the scout she'd met in Kansas City, leaning on the outer barrier of the bullpen. She waved at him, and, amazingly enough, he waved back, then beckoned her over.

"I'll be right back," she whispered to her brother, then made her way down the aisle and along the railing to the bullpen.

Stewart greeted her kindly. "Your boy's pitching great. Doing exactly what we wanted."

Caitlyn decided to let the "your boy" part pass. Everyone seemed to be under some kind of misapprehension about her and Eli, but she couldn't spend too much time setting the record straight. "I brought something from the candy shop. Do you think you would mind bringing it to the clubhouse? It's sort of a…birthday thing. But it's for everyone."

A doubtful look crossed Stewart's leathery face. "Sure thing, but you sure you want to do that? These boys will use any excuse to rib a guy. Especially a newbie."

"You don't have to say it's from me. Or from any girl. It could just be an anonymous birthday gift. I have a little something for you too. I think your wife will love it."

"In that case, bring it on. I'll make sure he gets it."

For the rest of the game, Caitlyn couldn't stop thinking about how Eli would react to her special birthday present…well, the first of her special birthday presents.

The next one would definitely not be delivered by someone else. And it wouldn't be in public in front of a bunch of wild and crazy ballplayers.

CHAPTER TEN

Eli pitched eight innings, gave up seven hits and only three runs, struck out four and came away with a 5-3 win. Not too shabby for a first start. He stayed in the dugout until the end of the game, his heart in his mouth as "Killer," the reliever, closed out the game. At the last pitch, he let out a bellow of triumph as the other Catfish clapped him on the back and offered high-fives.

"First win is an event," Dwight announced as the players began heading for the clubhouse. "Press is going to want to talk to you, so you better decide right now what you want to say. Thank your family? Grateful just to be here? Hoping you can help the team? Happy to be in Texas? Dream come true? Praise be to God?" He rattled off the possibilities.

"Um…all of the above?" Eli had never spoken to a reporter before.

"Sure. Why use one cliché when you can spill 'em all? You get in trouble, give me a wink and I'll ride to your rescue with my famous Dwight Conner charisma."

Trevor strode next to them. "In case you didn't notice, Nebraska, that was an attempt to share your spotlight. Back off, DC. He earned it."

Eli nearly flushed at those words from someone like Trevor Stark. Praise from a bona fide superstar like him really meant something.

Dwight pushed open the clubhouse door. "Whoa baby. What the hell is that?"

Trevor shouldered his way through the door and sniffed loudly. "Smells great in here. And that's not what I usually say when I walk into the clubhouse."

Eli stepped in next—and stopped dead at the sight of a giant bouquet on the bench next to his locker. A tall vase held about fifty long stems wrapped in silvery cellophane.

A wide blue ribbon held the stems upright, and a balloon
floated above the whole affair. In girly script it read,
"Happy Birthday!"

Caitlyn. This had Caitlyn written all over it. She loved
going all out for birthdays. But why…*why* did she have to
embarrass him in front of the other players? Flowers? Who
sent flowers to a ballplayer in a locker room? This wasn't
backstage at the opera, for Chrissake.

The sweaty players were gathering around, laughter
punctuating the usual post-game chatter.

"If a girl sends you flowers, she expects a proposal,"
said Bieberman wisely.

"You sure they aren't from his mother?" Ramirez
asked.

"Is there a card?"

"Yeah, it says, 'signed, crazed stalker.' Dwight strolled
closer. "Hang on one ever-loving second. You guys sure
those are flowers? They smell kind of funny." Dwight
leaned his face closer to take a sniff, then jumped back.
"Hey, Nebraska! Do you know who sent you these?"

Eli mumbled, "Pretty sure I do. She's a real sweetheart,
but she doesn't know about locker rooms and all that and—
"

"Because if you don't marry her, I will!"

"What?" Eli looked at Trevor, who took his turn
peering at the bouquet.

"You'll have to fight me for her," Trevor told Dwight.
"May the best man win."

"It's on." Dwight plucked one of the stems from the
vase and held it high. "Y'all know what this is?" He
brought it reverently to his nose and breathed deep.
"Bacon. She sent him a *bouquet of bacon.*"

The clubhouse erupted into applause. Eli shouldered
through the crowd to study the bouquet. Each "rose" was
actually a strip of bacon cleverly molded to look like a
flower from a distance. Caitlyn had made this bouquet for

him, who else could it be? He remembered the exact conversation in Kansas City when he'd jokingly suggested that more candy be made out of bacon.

Trevor jumped onto a bench, calling for quiet. "It's official. Not only did Nebraska just get his first win, but his girlfriend is a genius. Has anyone else ever gotten a bacon bouquet?"

A chorus of "no's" and laughter followed.

"And what's this?" Dwight called over the din. "A special note that says 'For Eli and the *rest of the Catfish*.' Line up, playas. Everyone who wants bacon, step this way. Eli, happy birthday, dude. *Damn* happy to have you here."

The rest of the Catfish seemed to agree, since they all clapped him on the back or shook his hand in between stuffing bacon into their mouths.

Caitlyn was...amazing.

In one stroke she'd made him laugh, touched his heart, and won over the entire Kilby Catfish crew.

And she was here in Kilby, and he was going to see her tonight.

He handed out bacon roses to all the players, while counting the minutes until he could hit the shower and get away from the guys. He might be the most popular person on the team at the moment, but all he wanted was to find his way to Caitlyn's side.

Unfortunately, they all decided they wanted to meet the genius behind the bacon bouquet, so they trooped outside en masse. There, outside the players' exit, waited Caitlyn, Ty, and Bryan in his wheelchair. It was a mark of what cool guys the Catfish were that no one looked at Bryan at all funny. They shook his hand, said nice things to Caitlyn, who turned pinker and pinker. A few recognized Ty from the Olympics. It was amazing how a simple thing like having friends show up at a game could bond him to his new team.

As a plan for the evening was being formed, Ty slung

an arm around his shoulders and drew him aside. "Here," he said, pressing a key card into his hand. "Top-floor suite at the best hotel in town. Happy birthday, my man."

Eli stared at the card. "Is this your hotel room?"

"Hotel *suite*," Ty corrected. "It even has a hot tub."

"What about you guys?"

"For now, I'm hitting the town with Bryan. Dude needs a little fun in his life. I'll give you a head's up when we're on our way back."

Eli felt himself turn various shades of red. Was Bryan okay with this plan? He gave his friend an uneasy look. Bryan was grinning like a jack-o'-lantern. Which made Eli think.

Ty and Bryan had brought Caitlyn here. Not only that, they'd sent her on that kidnapping trip to the tryout. Maybe there was more going on here than he'd realized at first.

And damn, he really wanted to spend some time alone with his girl.

Which was what she was, no matter how "casual" she wanted to keep things.

He pocketed the card key without a single other objection. Then he noticed that half the Catfish were talking to her, because who wouldn't instantly fall for a girl like her? And they were a good-looking bunch of guys, even he could see that. Trevor Stark was actually making a small mob of autograph-seekers wait while he raved about Cait's bacon roses.

Time to make a statement.

He waded into the crowd. Her eyes widened when she caught sight of him. He must look like some kind of pirate come to claim his prize.

Who cared what he looked like? He had a point to make. When he reached her side, he pulled her tight against him. Damn, she felt amazing, snugged up just right under his arm.

"Time's up, guys. Move along. Caitlyn has somewhere

she's supposed to be."

"I do?" She peered up at him, mischief in her bright eyes.

"Absolutely."

"Where am I supposed to be?"

He hugged her closer. "This is a good start, right here."

"Hmm, it's kind of public," she murmured.

His groin tightened at her implication.

"Eli, you coming to the Roadhouse?" Dwight Conner called as the throng of players began to disperse to their vehicles. "No one has to buy a drink on the night of their first win."

"Nah, I'll catch you next time."

No one seemed too surprised by that.

"Treat my friends right," he called after the Catfish.

"You know it," Dwight answered.

Next to him, Ramirez walked backwards for a moment to mouth something to Eli. *Married look.*

"What did he say?" Caitlyn asked.

"Oh, some baseball shit. Nothing interesting."

"Hm."

Now that they were finally alone, he turned her to face him. "Hey."

"Hey yourself." She tilted her head back, and he saw the uncertainty in her eyes. "I hope it's... I mean, the guys wanted to come and they insisted that I should too, probably because of my birthday expertise—"

"That's not the reason," he told her firmly.

She tugged her lower lip between her teeth. His mouth watered, since that's exactly the spot he wanted his mouth to be. "It's not?"

"The reason is that they knew seeing you would be the best birthday present they could think of. Well, one of the top three."

"*Top three?*" She pulled back, indignation chasing away her earlier uncertainty. "Oh really. What are the other two?"

"Winning my first start."

"Okay, that's one. And?"

He ran a thumb across her cheek. "I'll have to show you the third one somewhere more private." He poured every ounce of his lust for her into a long, smoldering look. She went beet red.

"I…uh…"

"Come on." He tugged her toward his vehicle, an old beater he'd picked up from a local car dealer who gave great deals to the Catfish. "Are you hungry? There's something I'm craving right now."

"What's that?"

"Room service."

Eli didn't let go of her hand the entire drive. He kept one hand on the wheel, the other firmly clasped around hers, resting on her thigh. Its warmth sank into every part of her being, until she felt like singing from pure happiness. It had all been so crazy—years of being his friend, months of crushing on him, one hot night, then instant separation. Being with him again now was like…floating on a cloud of cotton candy.

Hey, she was a candy-maker, what could she say?

When they reached the luxury hotel where Ty had booked them a suite, it was almost embarrassing how fast Eli parked the car and rushed them into the building. Except that she didn't care what anyone thought. She wanted him, now, for as long as they could get away with it, and she didn't care who knew.

Including the nice lady they shared the elevator with, the one who kept her eyes firmly on the door while Eli and Caitlyn snuck kisses behind her back.

"You kids have fun," she called when she finally reached her floor.

The doors closed again. "I plan to." Eli's voice

deepened. "How about you?"

"Absolutely." She plastered herself against him, unable to resist his touch one second longer. He hoisted her up and lifted her legs around his hips. *Closer, closer.* She couldn't get close enough. Too many clothes. Too many layers. Their lips converged at the exact same moment, as if following some invisible signal, in a blazing, perfect kiss.

Shivers raced along her skin, the excitement building so quickly it made her dizzy. His erection bulged against his jeans, pressing between her legs. His big hands cradled her ass, half on her shorts, half on the bare skin of her upper thighs. She let out a moan, unable to keep her delight to herself. Even such a simple touch felt incredibly, unbelievably good.

"I missed you," he told her, his lips moving softly against hers. "I wanted you here. I kept dreaming about it, and now here you are."

She snuggled even closer against him, soaking in the vibrations of his heartbeat. Eli was so hard, so solid, so hot, so muscular.

"I've been dreaming about this too. I guess it's like *Field of Dreams*. If you build it, they will come." *Field of Dreams* was her all-time favorite baseball movie; she'd seen it half a dozen times.

"Oh yeah? I could come right here and now," he growled.

"That is not what it means!" Her indignant words had to make their way between his kisses.

"I know what it means. I just want you. I can't think about anything else. Everything is going to sound dirty until I get you naked. Is this the longest freaking elevator ride in history?"

"You know how Ty rolls. Penthouse suite."

He groaned. "You had to say 'penthouse.' You just had to."

"That's not the kind of penthouse I meant!"

"I warned you. We'd better get in that room soon or I'll get you naked right here in this elevator."

Caitlyn yelped and tried to jump out of his arms, but he wouldn't let her. The elevator dinged, the doors sliding open. He strode into the hallway with her still firmly wrapped around his body. With truly impressive coordination, he extracted the card key from his pocket and whisked them into the room.

And stopped dead.

Satisfaction filled her as she watched the amazement spread across his face.

Eli was an easy guy to please. His favorite foods had been known to her since she'd watched her first football game with her brother and his friends. A feast of all those special items was arrayed on the glass table in the center of the suite. Buffalo wings with blue cheese dip, spicy guacamole, Triscuits and sliced cheddar, green olives stuffed with more blue cheese. Nothing could be simpler.

But from the look on his face, you'd think she'd whipped up a ten-course Cordon Bleu meal. "Wow."

Again, she tried to slip out of his grip, and again, he wouldn't let her.

"You did this?"

"Well, it wasn't Bryan or Ty. Unless they're trying to cut in on my birthday territory." She tried to laugh it off, but he looked so serious.

"No one's... I mean, I never expected..."

When he couldn't manage to finish his sentence, it finally sank in what he was trying to say. Eli had been taking care of everyone else for so long. When was the last time anyone had taken care of him?

"A lot of people really care about you, Eli," she said softly. "Not just me."

His arms tightened. "You care?"

"Yeah, like it's some big secret." She nudged him with her forehead. "I don't send flowers to just any boy."

That brought the smile back to his face. "You take the cake, Caitlyn. There's no one like you."

"The cake! I can't believe I almost forgot. Put me down." Her bossy tone got his attention and he finally released her.

"Where are you going?"

"Just trust me, okay?"

"Fine. But don't take long. I'll just be over here snacking."

"Go ahead and fuel up. You're going to need it." With a teasing wink, she skipped away from him. Oh, how she loved the way his eyes went dark with lust. This couldn't possibly be going any better.

CHAPTER ELEVEN

Eli was trying to figure out what he'd done to deserve someone as amazing as Caitlyn. All of his favorite foods in one place, at the same time. He popped an olive into his mouth. How had she known about all this? That was just the kind of person she was. She thought about other people. Tried to make them happy. That's why she made candy, and not just any candy—custom-designed candy. Made with love and thought specifically for each person.

Did she know how special she was? Not just to him, but in general? A guy could travel the world over, from Texas to San Diego and anywhere else, and not find someone as amazing as Cait. And there she'd been this whole time, while he'd been caught up in worry and hard work.

Was he the densest guy in Sapphire Falls?

"Why are you frowning, birthday boy?"

He looked up—then froze all over again.

Caitlyn stood in the middle of the room, wearing nothing but an apron. In one hand she held a bowl, in the other, a spatula.

His jaw dropped. "Wha…?"

"I happen to know you don't really like cake. Am I right?"

"Well…that's true." He'd always forced down the birthday cake people served at parties. He put it in the candy category. "But I'm sure any cake you make would be—"

She held up a hand, revealing one bare breast and a pink nipple winking at him. "No need to fudge the truth. You're not a cake guy. That's okay. Birthdays don't have to have cake. Anyway, the cake is just an excuse for the frosting. Remember that dream you had?" She tilted the bowl toward him.

Pink frosting.

He groaned, torn between lust and laughter. "You're trying to kill me, aren't you?"

She grinned back at him. Damn, she looked good in that apron. "Definitely not. We have some celebrating to do first."

"Since it's my birthday, you have to do what I say, right?"

She went a little pink. "I suppose."

"Turn around. I want to see how your ass looks in that apron."

She groaned, and didn't budge. "I'll tell you how it looks. Too big."

"No way. Come on. It's my birthday, you can't deny me."

Reluctantly, she turned, and he nearly came right then and there at the sight of her shapely rear bare underneath the big ribbon she'd tied in the back. "You are the sexiest thing I've ever seen." He came close and reverently caressed her ass. Sleek curves tempted his fingers and made his cock harden. She quivered under his touch and her breath caught.

"Put the spatula down and hand me the bowl," he told her. She did as he said. He pulled her against him, so her back nested against his front, his rock-hard erection making its presence known.

"You do think I'm sexy," she breathed, almost as if she hadn't believed it.

"I do. Every part of you. This part right up there with the rest." Again he stroked her behind. "Turn around now."

With satisfaction, he saw the flush of arousal already turning her chest pink. This was something he'd discovered during their first night together. When Caitlyn got turned on, it showed in her creamy skin, in her sensitive nipples, in the widening pupils of her hazel eyes. If he knew his girl— and he was just starting to, really—she was halfway to an orgasm already. He could slip his hand under that apron right now and get her off.

But he had to take advantage of the frosting first.

Gently, he tugged at the ribbon of the apron so it fell to the floor. He wanted her entirely naked, pink and flushed and delicious as one of her cupcakes.

"Best birthday present ever," he murmured.

He dipped his finger into the bowl and painted a letter above her breasts. A big letter I, with the bottom part spanning the distance from nipple to nipple.

She probably didn't realize it was a letter. She probably thought it was a random design. And that was fine. But so much emotion pounded in his heart, he had to let it out. Slowly, he added another word. Four letters, one starting at the left nipple, one ending at the right. L.O.V.E.

She half-closed her eyes, which hazed over with pleasure. With her skin so warm, almost feverish, the frosting started to melt right away. So he quickly added the last word, "you," followed by an exclamation point ending in a dot on her clit.

She gasped. Because of how it felt, or what he'd written, he wasn't sure. But since the pink sugar was starting to run down her body, he lapped it off her nipples, her natural sweetness enhanced by the pink icing. Something about the way the frosting ran down her body was outrageously erotic. He knelt on the floor to capture the end of his exclamation point. Swirling his tongue to chase down every bit of runaway frosting, he pulled a cry from her lips. He gripped her ass to bring her tight against him and leave no room for escape from his tongue. More icing dripped down her body, making its way through the thatch of curls protecting her mound. He lapped up every bit, savoring each tremor and jump of her hips.

"Oh God, Eli. That feels so good, don't stop, I'm going to…oh my God…"

He smiled against her sweet clit. One thing he really loved about Caitlyn was how vocal she got when she was ready to come. She actually got kind of bossy about it. She threw herself into her orgasms the way she did everything else. Passionately. And he was more than happy to help her get there. He increased the pressure on her hot little nub in an enticing, teasing dance that made her inner thighs quiver.

"Eli!" She practically screamed at him.

Okay, sweetheart, he thought. *I'm here to please.* And he brought his thumb against her swollen flesh and pressed just so. She exploded into his mouth. He kept lapping and pressing as huge spasms shook her body and soft mutters poured into the room. "Yes...oh my God...feels so good... Eli... Eli..."

That's right. Say my name, he thought fiercely. *Because you're mine, and you'd better not ever forget it.*

Her hands gripped his shoulders, tugging him upwards in a clear message. *Get inside me. Now.*

No problem.

He scooped her up and brought her to the bed, where he could spread open her legs and bury himself in her warm, welcoming body. Thank God she'd gone on the pill after Kansas City. When she'd told him, all he could think about was thrusting into her with no barrier, nothing between them, just her heat, her wetness, her tight, tight sheath. And now she was here, it was real, and... He slowly entered her, the rush of pleasure almost too much. He clenched every muscle hard to keep from coming too soon.

"God Caitlyn. I can't—"

"Do it." She arched her hips up, tightening her body so he no longer really had any say in it.

He came. Hard and long. Pumping, straining, pouring himself into her body. And she met him thrust for thrust, his hot, sweet Candy-girl.

The last thing she whispered, right before he drifted off into a drugged, satisfied slumber, was, "Me too."

He wasn't sure exactly what she meant, but then again,

nothing really mattered at that moment besides the feel of her in his arms and the silky weight of her head against his chest.

ৎৼৡ৶

When things went crazy, people often said that life had thrown them a curveball.

Caitlyn really thought what was going on for her was more like Eli's knuckleball—unpredictable and fast. Really fast. Her head was still spinning from watching the latest pitch whiz by.

Eli loved her.

Caitlyn had known exactly what he'd written on her skin in pink frosting. She could still feel the letters he'd traced with his calloused finger.

I love you.

Exclamation point.

And not just any exclamation point, either, but the most erotic one she could imagine. She might not ever be able to look at that particular type of punctuation mark again without blushing.

But there was no denying the truth—she was in love too.

She had the feeling that Eli thought he was being kind of secretive and mysterious. And he never said it out loud. She wasn't sure why, but whatever the reason, she couldn't let him go to sleep without letting him know that his message had been heard.

I love you.

Way ahead of you, Eli.

He'd fallen asleep on the king-size bed, sprawled out every which way, bits of pink frosting smeared on his torso. The sugar was starting to tighten on her skin, kind of like a body scrub. She should really rinse everything off, but it felt so good to lie next to Eli like this. So perfect. It was

108

everything she'd ever dreamed about. The only thing that would make it even more wonderful would be if three children were sleeping in the other room. Or climbing into bed with them, eager for the day's fun of playing catch or baking cookies. Really, that's all it would take to make her happy.

Well, and maybe a puppy.

But it was all too much, too fast. Wasn't it?

Then Eli sighed in his sleep, rolled toward her, and reached out to rest his hand on her stomach. The heavy, warm touch heated a lot more than her stomach and it wasn't in the hot, lusty way she was used to his touch affecting her. She just felt...warm. All over. Especially in her chest. Right over her heart.

It might be fast, but it felt really, really good.

And suddenly she knew one thing for certain—she wasn't going to spend her time with Eli in Kilby *sleeping*. She could sleep in Sapphire Falls. When she was alone.

She stubbornly refused to go any further down the track of that train of thought.

Instead, she studied Eli.

She wasn't sure how deep a sleeper he was. Or, more specifically, how to best wake him up.

She stretched, her legs rubbing against his.

He sighed again and rolled closer, wedging his leg between hers.

Okay, that was nice. But he was still asleep.

She stretched again, arms over head, giving a little groan at the same time.

Eli's fingers flexed on her stomach and then spread again and slipped slightly lower. Caitlyn didn't *mind*, of course, but he was definitely still sleeping. He was breathing slow and deep, with just the slightest rattle of a soft snore.

Caitlyn arched her back and poked her big toe into his calf. Firmly but not too hard.

That got a little more movement out of him. He shifted his leg but somehow also cuddled closer, bringing his head against her chest. Caitlyn froze. Okay, that was *really* nice. Especially when he moved his head, as if trying to get comfortable on his new "pillow." The light scruff on his chin rubbing on the sensitive skin shot tingles over her breasts and made her nipples pebble.

This time the little moan that escaped from her was less intentional.

He was *really* asleep and she was getting worked up.

She weighed her options. She could go to sleep. But she didn't want to sleep. She could poke him harder, or pinch him, or shout "Eli!" and wake him up. But she had a better idea. She could really enjoy waking him up.

Caitlyn moved her arm, circling Eli's back and spreading her palm over the hot, firm muscles along his spine. She ran it up and down, loving the feel of his smooth skin and strong body. Then she let it travel lower. To the magnificent ass that looked so, so good in baseball pants. She squeezed lightly and was rewarded with a soft groan from him.

She tipped her head but saw he was still asleep, his gorgeous mouth centimeters from her nipple. In fact, if he tipped his chin just a bit…

But instead, he suddenly took a deep breath and rolled to his back, trapping her hand underneath him.

She almost giggled. It wasn't that she minded having her hand stuck between the mattress and one of her favorite body parts of his. Besides, when he was on his back, the sheet slipped slightly, exposing his rock-hard abs and the lines on either side that every woman on Facebook agreed made girls stupid.

The sheet clung to another of her favorite parts and she was gratified to see that it wasn't entirely immune to her touch, even if Eli's other brain was asleep.

Since she couldn't go far in the other direction with her

hand underneath him—darn it anyway—she slid closer. She put her hand on his chest to start. For a moment, she held it there, feeling the rise and fall of his breaths and watching his face.

She really did love him. If she hadn't known it before, the soul-deep happiness she'd felt for him when he first got the call from Kilby, and then the intense pride she'd experienced for him today at the ballpark, had cemented it. No matter what it meant for her, she wanted him to be happy and successful and confident and to see all his dreams come true. Because she loved him.

Caitlyn moved her hand so it was resting over his heart and she absorbed the feel of the strong, steady beats there before stealing down over his rib cage to the ridges of the ab muscles. She traced each one with her fingertip, marveling at the power there.

Then her fingertip trailed lower, following the path of the silky hair that ran from his belly button to his—

Suddenly she found herself scooped up on top of him.

"Oomph," was her sexy response.

Eli grinned up at her. "Taking advantage of me while I sleep?"

She blinked innocently. "I was trying to wake you up."

"Uh-huh." He slid her up his body until her breast was right above his mouth. "And to think I held off on this because I really thought you were just stretching." He fastened his lips around her nipple.

Caitlyn gasped. It took her a minute—and Eli letting go of her nipple—for her to realize what he'd said. "You were awake when you were lying with your head on my chest?"

He grinned unapologetically. "Let's take a shower. This icing is getting itchy."

"But I thought…"

"That I was going to make love to you until you're a little pile of quivering goo that can only manage three words? Yep, that's exactly what I'm going to do."

Even though she was still draped over him like a favorite blanket, Eli managed to sit up and swing his legs over the side of the bed, holding her to him. Then he slid his hands under her ass and stood, striding toward the bathroom.

Caitlyn's heart was pounding and she wasn't sure if it was from that delicious display of alpha strength, the promise of lovemaking in the shower, or the three words he'd alluded to.

He let her slide down his body until her feet touched the bathmat and he leaned in to turn on the shower.

Okay, it was all of the above.

"What three words would those be?" she asked lightly.

I love you. Say it, Eli. Tell me. Say it out loud.

He gave her a grin. But instead of the madly-in-love grin that would flip her heart over, it was a bad-boy grin that still made every inch of her body tingle.

"Eli you're amazing."

She blinked at him. Then she laughed. She couldn't help it. "I can already tell you that," she said honestly.

He put his hands on her waist and lifted her into the shower, then joined her, crowding her up against the wall under the warm water spray. With his big, hard body against hers, both growing hotter and slipperier with the water, he said, "Then how about these three—more, harder and yes?"

She wrapped her arms around his neck. They would get to the I love yous. He'd written it in icing after all. Everyone knew once you put it in icing, you couldn't take it back. It was as good as Happy Birthday or It's a Girl! Icing mattered.

"Oh, I can manage those three." She kissed his cheek. "And maybe an *I need you* thrown in there." She kissed his lips. "And an *I want you*." She put her lips against his ear. "And a *please fuck me*."

He growled, picked her up and went about making her

use all of those word trios. A few times.

When they finally made it out of the bathroom, Caitlyn felt boneless.

And hungry.

Her stomach growled as she climbed back up onto the bed.

"I heard that," Eli told her. "Let me grab you some stuff from the other room."

But she had a better idea. At least, she hoped it was a better idea.

"Let's go out."

He stopped in the doorway and turned back. "Out?"

She nodded, clutching the ends of the huge, fluffy white towel between her breasts. "I'd love a tour of Kilby. That way, when…" She trailed off.

He wrote I love you on you in icing, she reminded herself. Still, she felt presumptuous.

"That way what?" he asked, walking back to the bed.

She bit her bottom lip, watching him. But he just looked curious. She took a breath. "That way, when we're talking on the phone and you tell me where you are or where you were that day, I'll be able to picture it."

Something flickered in his eyes. But finally he said, "Okay, let's do it. I'd love to show you around."

"Really?"

"Sure. It's kind of a fun town. I haven't been here long, but I've already heard some crazy stories. And yeah," he nodded, "I get it. When I'm texting you and I know you're at work, I picture the shop. Or when I know you're at home, I picture your house." He leaned in and braced his hands on the mattress, causing her to tip toward him. "And when we're sexting and I know you're in bed, I can picture your bedroom."

Caitlyn felt her body heating. Again. The power this guy had over her hormones was astonishing. "We, um…" She licked her lips and loved how his eyes darkened as he watched the motion. "We haven't sexted."

"No. Not yet."

So being away from him wouldn't be *all* bad.

He leaned in closer, his lips nearly touching hers. "And when I was getting off thinking about you, I was picturing you spread out on that big table Adrianne has in the back room at her shop, with all the sugar and syrups and colored sprinkles. Just so you know."

Then he leaned back and Caitlyn had to jerk herself upright to keep from falling over.

She was never going to be able to roll out cookies or make truffles on that back table again without getting hot and bothered.

From the smug look on Eli's face, he knew it too. And had told her all of that very intentionally.

"Yes. Let's go find some places for me to imagine going down on my knees, unzipping you and taking you in my mouth while *I'm* getting off."

Eli made that sexy, deep growling noise that she loved so much and started to reach for her, but she scooted back on the bed quickly, laughing. "No way, Hotshot, you started this."

He narrowed his eyes. "Okay fine. But I'm going to be sure you're *remembering* being bent over and taken hard from behind somewhere in this town while you're getting off too."

She tingled the entire time she got dressed, put her hair up in a messy bun and slipped into her shoes. She hadn't seen more than the hotel and the ballpark and Caitlyn already loved Kilby, Texas. With a passion.

CHAPTER TWELVE

Eli couldn't describe exactly what he was feeling as he drove through the historic downtown district of Kilby with Caitlyn by his side.

It felt good. It felt...right. But it was even more than that. Like déjà vu about something that hadn't happened yet.

"Kilby's a little bigger than Sapphire Falls," he said. "But it's still a small town and everyone knows everything about everybody else."

"The curse and the blessing," Caitlyn said.

That it was.

"They've got a Starbucks here but I haven't been yet," he said. "I have, however, been to Sacred Grounds." He pointed at a darkened storefront. "It's an organic, New Age kind of café."

Caitlyn laughed. "How's it compare to Dottie's coffee?" she asked.

Strangely, Eli's heart squeezed a little at the name of the diner in Sapphire Falls. He already missed the fried green tomatoes. "Better," he admitted.

Caitlyn wrinkled her nose. "Okay, I can believe that. But there's no way they have better muffins than we do."

Adrianne Riley had the best muffins in six counties. Probably more, but no one had taste-tested farther out than that. "Adrianne's are definitely better," Eli agreed. "Definitely."

"Well, thank goodness. If they had muffins better than Adrianne's I'd have to move here."

Eli froze.

Caitlyn seemed to as well.

The weird déjà vu thing hit him at the same time the thought *I want her here so fucking bad* went skating through his mind. That was what that strange, feels-like-a-

115

memory-but-it's-not-yet thing was—he *wanted* to have driven down Main Street Kilby with Caitlyn beside him a hundred times in the past.

He wanted to be to the point where he could look back and remember the first time they'd done this. While they did it for the hundredth time.

Eli forced himself to take a deep breath and relax his grip on the steering wheel.

She laughed a second later, but the sound seemed forced. "I'm glad Adrianne's are still better. I hate packing."

He let it go.

For now.

"This is the road that leads to the Roadhouse, the main…social spot, I guess."

Beer, bluegrass and blue jeans. That was the Roadhouse. He'd only been once. So far. The team did like to hang out there. But he hadn't really let himself kick back. He was still getting to know the guys, trying to make a good impression and…well, old habits died hard. Back home, he'd go to the Come Again with friends, of course. But he usually kept to one beer and was home well before midnight. He had responsibilities, he had people depending on him. And he had to get up early in the morning.

But here…well, here his main responsibility was throwing strikes. It was strange to think that he could go out and stay out and have fun. He didn't have to check in on the hardware store every hour, even though he'd been calling every day to make sure nothing slipped through the cracks. He didn't have to go in early to do inventory. He didn't have to stay late doing inventory either.

It was really nice. And he felt really guilty about that.

"Is it like the Come Again?" Caitlyn asked of Kilby's bar.

He laughed. "A little rougher around the edges. Live music and rowdy ballplayers But beer, fried food and…yeah, basically."

She smiled. "You want to go in?"

He thought about that. There was a part of him that did. He hadn't spun a girl around a dance floor in a long time. He hadn't even bought a girl a drink in a long time. He definitely hadn't made out with a girl in a dark corner of a bar in a long time. He'd love to walk into the Roadhouse from now on and think about dancing and drinking and making out with Caitlyn.

But he'd be thinking about her anyway. He would be *not* dancing, drinking or making out with anyone else because of her.

This was his new home, his team, his dream. And she was his girl. His…love. Another dream. Did he want to combine the two?

Yeah, kind of.

But not yet.

Tonight he wanted to imprint memories of her all over town, not just with the team.

Even before he'd seen her in the stands and before the bacon bouquet in the locker room, he'd thought of her whenever he took the mound. She was part of all of it. She was the reason he was here. Literally. She'd kidnapped him. But she was a part of this because of her belief in him.

He'd been on the mound a thousand times before he'd had Caitlyn in his life. But now—everything, even the best things, were better. And it was probably crazy but he wanted her to touch everything else. He had a feeling even the best burrito he'd had would be better with Caitlyn there.

He already had her touch on the ballpark, stands and locker room. Now he needed her everywhere else.

He stopped the truck and reached over and cupped the back of her neck. He pulled her close and kissed her deep and hot and sweet.

"There's more to Kilby than the Roadhouse," he said after he'd fully tasted her. "Our tour is just starting."

117

"Okay." She seemed perfectly happy with that answer.

He continued down Main. Kilby was a charming mix of old brickwork and Spanish-style stucco architecture. The biggest landmarks were an old fort, a sort of wannabe Alamo, and a statue of Colonel Kilby on a rearing horse. But he didn't care about either of those at the moment. "There's the flower shop where I plan to send you flowers from," he said, pointing to the shop with the sunshine-yellow awning.

She smiled at that and he imagined that was the same smile that would be on her face when she got the flowers at the Sweet Shop and read the mushy card he'd include. Because it would have to be mushy. Caitlyn deserved flowers with mushy cards attached.

"You can order flowers for delivery online, you know," she said.

He nodded. Not that he'd ever done it. In fact, he couldn't remember the last time he'd sent a girl flowers. Had he *ever* sent a girl flowers? The best he could think of was the corsage he'd given his prom date. He hadn't been all about romance back then. Or ever. He'd been all about baseball. Period.

His chest felt a little tight as he again realized that with Caitlyn, he could have it all—baseball and romance.

He took her hand and lifted it to kiss the back. "I know. But I want to go into that shop right there, pick out flowers I know will make you light up, and dictate the card in person."

Her smile turned even sweeter. "Sounds good to me."

He kept ahold of her hand as he continued down the street. "And there's the grocery store where I'll buy the ingredients to make you dinner the next time you come down."

"Ooh, what will it be?" Her light tone indicated that she was expecting him to say something simple like spaghetti with sauce from a jar.

He grinned. He had a few surprises for Miss Caitlyn. "Teriyaki salmon, roasted asparagus and parmesan risotto."

She was completely quiet at that. He looked over to find her staring at him with her mouth open.

"What?"

"Seriously?"

He gave her a wink. "Seriously. And Candy-girl, I'm even going to make you dessert. You might be the pro, but I've got some skills."

"What will dessert be?"

"A surprise."

Caitlyn turned slightly on her seat. "If you say crème brûlée, I'll love you forever."

Her teasing words slammed into him.

I want that.

God, he wanted that.

He swallowed hard. "Crème brûlée it is then."

He'd look up how to make that first thing tomorrow. After Cait and Ty and Bryan left. Eli was shocked by how much he hated the idea of saying goodbye to her. He worked on not squeezing her hand too hard.

They kept driving. "Okay, so here's the café where I'll bring you for breakfast the next morning." He paused. "Make that brunch. No, lunch."

She laughed. "They don't do good breakfasts?"

He hadn't actually been there for breakfast yet. But that wasn't the issue. "I'll be keeping you up too late to make it out of bed before lunch," he said with a grin.

Her grin matched his when he glanced over and his chest and his cock tightened simultaneously.

Hell, they might not be able to do more than get a pizza delivered.

"Here's the post office," she said, as they rolled past. "This is where you'll pick up the care packages I send."

His heart thumped. God, how could he *not* love her?

119

"What kinds of stuff will be in these packages?" he asked, pulling up in front of the building.

"Cookies," she said. "Of course. Copies of the *Sapphire Falls Times*. Some nuts and bolts because you'll miss them." She gave him a grin. "Bacon cupcakes."

"That all sounds ama— Hang on," he said, as the last two works sunk in. "Bacon *cupcakes?*"

She nodded. "Maple cupcakes with pieces of real bacon in the frosting."

Damn. "You send those and *I'll* love *you* forever."

The words were not an accident. He wanted to tell her. He wanted her to know what he'd written in pink icing on her body. He wanted to tell the *world*.

"Well, then I wonder how you'll feel when you see the dirty notes I'll include," she told him with a mischievous smile.

"Like the luckiest man in the world," Eli said gruffly.

He leaned in and kissed her again. By the time he'd finished, she had the front of his shirt crumpled in both fists.

"Let's go have ice cream," he said, when he'd pulled back.

"Ice cream?" She blinked up at him. "Is that code for something else?"

He laughed and brushed her hair back from her cheek. He loved how much she wanted him too. "No. I want to buy you an ice cream sundae. I know it sounds crazy and cheesy and dumb but that seems like a date thing, a boyfriend-girlfriend thing. We've never dated. We jumped from friends to lovers and we don't really need to get to know each other or share a lot of stories about our pasts or our families, but I want some of that sweet stuff too."

She shook her head, her expression confused and touched at the same time. "I'm a sure thing, you know."

He chuckled and ran a thumb over her cheek. "I want you to know that the sweet, romantic stuff is a sure thing too."

She sighed, the sound a happy, contented one. "So, no taking me from behind somewhere semi-public in Kilby?"

Lust rushed through him. But there was something else too, something softer. Love.

"I didn't say that, did I?" He gave her a wicked grin and began mentally cataloging all of the places he knew of that might work as he drove to Scoop, Kilby's most popular ice cream shop.

He hadn't been in Kilby long enough to really know. Over the back of the couch in the hotel suite seemed fine with him.

But ice cream first. Caitlyn Murray deserved to be wooed a little.

Ten minutes later, Eli had decided that buying Caitlyn ice cream was the worst idea ever. She scooped up a spoonful of vanilla ice cream and caramel topping and proceeded to lick the creamy mixture from her spoon. Slowly. Seductively. Her eyes on Eli's the whole time.

He took a huge bite of his own ice cream with hot fudge, hoping to cool off a little. Turned out that wanting a woman more than his next breath made romantic wooing a chore. He wanted to grab her and the ice cream and head back to the hotel for a sweet, sticky snack. He was certain that her skin would taste even better with caramel on it than the ice cream did.

"No chocolate, huh?" he asked, trying to keep to friendly, innocuous talk rather than telling her all the things he'd rather she be doing with her tongue.

Caitlyn swallowed her bite. "Chocolate is great. Caramel's just better." She grinned.

Caramel is better. Noted.

Though he could make her like hot fudge *a lot*. Or strawberry. Or marshmallow…

"Hot fudge is your go-to though?" she asked.

He watched the tip of her tongue pick up a drop of ice

cream from her bottom lip.

"Eli?"

He looked up into her eyes. "Huh?"

"Hot fudge? That's your favorite?"

"Caitlyn."

"Yes?"

He gave her a half grin. "That's my favorite flavor. Caitlyn."

Her cheeks turned a little pink but her smile was huge. "Not an ice cream topping."

"You're right. You would be under the ice cream. How about we take some to go and I'll show you how Caitlyn flavoring really goes with anything."

She grinned and licked at her spoon again, nearly missing the drizzle of caramel. Which would have landed on her right breast. He could easily imagine the caramel sliding down the sweet mound to her nipple. He'd become a fast fan of caramel too.

"I'd like to take that spoon and—"

"Hey, Eli."

He sat up straight and focused on the waitress standing next to their table.

Crap. She hadn't waited on them tonight, but Eli knew he knew her from somewhere, he just couldn't place it.

"Is this Caitlyn?"

He looked at Caitlyn in surprise. But she didn't seem to know the woman either.

"Uh, yes. My girlfriend. From back home in Sapphire Falls."

"Yeah, you're the one that makes the Cracker Jacks, right?" the waitress asked.

Caitlyn laughed. "You know about that?"

"Stewart is my dad," the woman said. "I'm Jill." She offered Caitlyn her hand.

Jill. Right. The scout's daughter. She'd stopped by practice the other day.

"Dad was raving about your stuff," Jill said. "He was hoping you would make it on a regular basis."

Caitlyn blushed. "How nice. It was just a recipe I was playing with."

"Well, he said I should talk to you about selling it in here. I own this shop and we're always looking for new treats. Do you do anything else that's baseball themed?"

Caitlyn gave Eli a surprised glace but she nodded. "Um, yes. I do dipped strawberries and then decorate them to look like baseballs. And cookies in various shapes, of course—bats and gloves and bases. And then there's my Take Me Out to the Ballgame cupcakes."

Her eyes were sparkling as she spoke and Eli felt a warmth spread in his chest.

Pride. He was proud of her. Her skills in the kitchen were well known in Sapphire Falls but she deserved to be known beyond their tiny hometown.

"Wow, tell me about those," Jill said.

"The cupcake batter has a light ale in it and then the frosting is peanut butter with crushed roasted peanuts on top."

Jill's eyes widened. Eli's felt his doing the same. Holy crap those sounded amazing.

"I'm sold," Jill said with enthusiasm. "Those would be a huge hit. We could even talk about setting up a little stand at the park."

Caitlyn looked over at Eli again. He gave her a wink.

"Really?" she asked Jill.

"Yeah, let's talk business. Put together a proposal and email it to me." Jill leaned over and scribbled her email address and phone number on a napkin.

Caitlyn picked it up and stared. "But…" She looked up. "You don't even know me."

"But you're with Eli. Eli's a Catfish. That means you're one of us," Jill said. "And when Eli moves up to San Diego, we'll figure something out. Maybe we can get our mail-order stuff and website finally set up."

"When Eli... But..."

Eli jumped in when Caitlyn continued to stumble over her words. "Thank you so much, Jill. That's really great of you."

"Well, I know you're gonna be a big star and make millions but I thought your girl might want something to do when she moves down here," Jill said with a grin.

"Move? But... Eli...," Caitlyn started again.

Eli couldn't help but chuckle, even though he didn't love her obvious shock over the idea of moving down here to be with him.

"Thanks, Jill," Eli said.

"You bet. I'll make some calls. I'll be waiting to hear from you," she told Caitlyn before she moved off.

Eli looked over at Caitlyn. He gave her a wink. "That your catfish impression?"

Caitlyn had been watching Jill walk away. She swung back to face him. "Huh?"

"With your eyes wide and your mouth hanging open, you look a little bit like a catfish."

She snapped her mouth shut.

He chuckled.

"Sorry about that," she said. "People are assuming a lot."

Was she embarrassed by the idea that people were assuming they were so serious she would soon be moving down here and eventually going to San Diego—God willing—with him?

"I don't mind that people are assuming we're going to end up together, Cait. I want you here. As much as possible. All the time, if possible."

She swallowed hard. "I've always wanted to have my own shop."

"Yeah?" It occurred to Eli that, while he'd known Caitlyn most of his life, and knew all about how she'd grown up and her friends and family, he didn't know about her plans, *her* dreams.

She'd been all about his dreams. She's *taken him* to his dreams. She'd never stopped believing. And pushing.

But he didn't know what she wanted.

"You've always wanted to own a bakery?"

She shrugged. "I think I always assumed I'd do desserts in a big fancy restaurant, actually. But I had thought about owning my own restaurant. A dessert-only place. I was going to call it Just Desserts." She gave him an adorably abashed smile.

"That's awesome," Eli said. "I...never knew that."

And suddenly he felt like kind of an ass. She knew everything about him, everything about what he wanted.

Okay, maybe she didn't know *everything* about how he felt about her. And he most definitely wanted her. But she would know. Soon.

She tipped her head with a little smile. "How would you have known?"

Because he could have *asked* her. He could have taken her out on a date and *talked* to her. He could have taken her out on a dozen dates. He could have not assumed he already knew her and knew what was important to her. He could have not gotten so wrapped up in his own stuff over the past few weeks and done more than flirted with her via text.

He reached across the table and took her hand. "Tell me about it now."

"There's nothing to tell now."

"What do you mean?"

"I was in Denver at culinary school. I had just finished up and was ready to start my first job. My plan was to start there, learn the business, network, and start saving money and working on a business plan."

"So your plan is to go back to Denver?" His gut knotted at the thought.

Did she want Denver? Her restaurant? Her baking and candy making? If so, could he let her go without an embarrassing display of begging? If she was ready and willing to leave Sapphire Falls, he wanted her here, in Kilby.

But that wasn't fair.

She shook her head. "I don't really have a plan."

"But you have a dream."

Her eyes studied his for a long moment. "I do have a dream."

"So tell me about that."

"Three kids."

Eli wasn't sure what that meant. "What?"

"Three kids. A dog. A fireplace to cuddle in front of. A kitchen with a big table and dinner together every night. A refrigerator covered in drawings and artwork that my kids made. Big Christmases. Huge birthdays. Summer vacations. Bedtime stories. Romantic weekends away while the kids stay at grandma and grandpa's. Falling asleep in my husband's arms every night and waking up to his face every morning. A fiftieth wedding anniversary." She took a deep breath. "That's my dream."

Eli's breath lodged in his throat as if he'd swallowed a huge glob of glue.

It was weird, but listening to her list off the things she wanted, and looking into her eyes as she talked about it, a sense of rightness came over him.

That dream completely fit the sweet, giving, beautiful woman in front of him. He *loved* her dream.

And he wanted to be a part of it.

"Thank you for telling me," he said softly, stroking the back of her knuckles with his thumb.

"Thank you for wanting to know."

He was so glad she could tell that he really did want to know.

"So where do you want this dream to come true? If

your heart's not set on Denver?" he asked.

She sighed. "Sapphire Falls. I guess."

No. That *didn't* feel right. He loved his hometown. He knew she did too. And someday he'd go back, after he retired, after he'd had a chance to chase his dream clear to the end. Or rather, after he'd chased this part of his dream. Because now that Caitlyn had shared her dream, he knew that she'd just told him the rest of his.

Caitlyn would be content back in Sapphire Falls someday too. But her dream could, and should, start right now. Here. With him.

"Bryan is doing great," he said. He knew that her brother was actually what was keeping her in Sapphire Falls.

"Bryan is doing better," she said.

"He's..." Eli trailed off, not sure what exact word he was looking for.

"Bryan," she filled in.

He laughed and nodded. "He's Bryan. He's tough, he's stubborn and he finds a way to make it all work out."

A sadness came into her eyes. "He can't make this work out, Eli. The injury is permanent. He's improved, the doctors think he can still make some gains. But he's never going to get back to where he was."

Eli took a second just to breathe. He knew all of that. But he hated hearing it. It was hard to believe that Bryan Murray was permanently sidelined. Bryan had always been larger than life. He took risks, he went hard and fast. And he had a hell of a good time doing it.

That was the thing. Bryan seemed to still be, if not having fun, at least adjusted to everything. Bryan faced everything head-on. Good and bad. His competitive spirit and his natural ability to see negatives and setbacks simply as reasons to try again and go harder, had brought him a long way.

It was Caitlyn who hadn't adjusted.

"You know how I know he's going to be okay? He's been flirting with Tessa," Eli said.

"He's been teasing about flirting with Tessa," Caitlyn said. But that did get a little bit of a smile. "He's not getting anywhere."

Eli laughed. "Because Tess knows that a wheelchair doesn't change Bryan's player status."

That made her smile a bit bigger. "Yeah, probably."

"For sure. Because it doesn't. That wheelchair has become his *best* play in a lot of ways. Have you seen him out with the girls?"

Caitlyn rolled her eyes. "No. He behaves himself when I'm around. At least mostly. He's definitely gotten more than his share of pies and casseroles and lots of free coffee and beer."

Eli nodded. "Exactly. And I *have* seen him with the girls. He's still Bryan. And with the guys. With everyone."

She shook her head. "Not everyone. My mom...she's in such deep denial about his injury, and he feeds it. He never lets on about how bad it is. He lets her think it's all fine. He never uses his chair over there. Which means, when he does need family, it's on me."

"And you think that you need to stay in Sapphire Falls for Bryan, forever?" Eli asked.

But of course she did. Caitlyn was one of the most loving, generous people he knew.

"Someone has to be there for him."

"Bryan has tons of friends, the rest of your family...he can hire the specific help."

She pressed her lips together and tried to pull her hand away.

He hung on. He couldn't let her get away. He was pushing, he knew that. And he understood that he was asking her to make a choice...between him and her brother. And that if he pushed too hard, he would lose. He couldn't lose.

"Okay," he said, still holding her hand. "Then tell me that you can come and visit for extended periods of time. You can come down here and stay for a couple of weeks at a time."

She chewed on her bottom lip.

"Bryan will be okay for a couple of weeks at a time, right? People will step up and help him." It wasn't what he wanted. He wanted her all the time, fully his. But he would take what he could get.

"You would really want that?" she asked. "That would be enough?"

"No. Yes. If it's that or nothing, I choose that."

"Really?"

He laughed lightly. It was time she knew this for sure. "I love you, Caitlyn. I've probably loved you for a long time. But I fell for you fully when you tricked me into your car and forced me to try out with the Catfish. You are the most amazing person I know, and yes, I love you and I want you here as much as possible."

She was staring at him, her hand tight around his. "Wow. I could...yeah... Be here. More. Often."

"Hey, I have some news." Jill was beside the table again.

They both jumped and looked up at her.

"Everyone's really excited about selling your stuff here."

"That was...fast," Caitlyn said.

"It's good to be the boss," Jill said.

"Right."

"I'd love to have stuff by the next game. So I just need to know if you're going to send it down here for me or if you're going to stay and make it all here."

Caitlyn cleared her throat. "Um, I...don't..." She looked at Eli for help again.

This time he shook his head. "*You* gotta answer this one, Cait. You going back or you staying here?"

Emotions flickered through her eyes. Eli wanted to take it back. He wasn't at all sure about what she was going to say and he was afraid that pushing would only force her toward the answer he didn't want to hear.

"I'm going back," she said softly.

Eli's heart dropped. Disappointment coursed through him.

He knew this was all too fast. It was too soon. He'd known better than to push.

"But I can come back. Midweek. I'll get everything made and then..." She looked at Eli. "I'll stay for a while."

"A while?" he repeated.

"Yeah. A while." She looked from him to Jill. "I can spend a couple of weeks a month here. We'll work it out."

"Awesome!" Jill gave her a big grin. "My dad will insist this was all his idea and will want us to all tell him how brilliant he is. Just so you know."

Caitlyn smiled and nodded. "Got it."

Eli had no trouble telling Stewart he was brilliant either. If he was part of bringing Caitlyn back to Kilby, or making it easier for her to visit as much as possible, then Stewart was one of Eli's favorite people.

Jill moved off and Caitlyn turned back to Eli. "I—"

Her phone rang just then, but she reached into her purse to silence it without looking at it.

"I love you too," she said. "I've loved you forever. I—"

As Eli was trying to get his heart to beat again after hearing what he'd been craving, her phone rang again.

She gave a little growl and glanced down and frowned. "Who is it?"

"Ty."

"You can pick up," Eli told her.

She silenced it again and shook her head. "They're probably in jail or something. They can wait."

He chuckled. "Cait, I heard what I needed to hear. You love me. That's all I need to know. We have forever now."

Her eyes widened and then her whole face, her whole body, seemed to soften. "That's so—"

Her phone rang again.

"Oh for—" She picked it up and swiped the screen. "What?"

Eli saw the immediate change in her expression and the tension grip her body. He leaned in.

"Where?" she asked Ty. She paused to listen. "We're on our way."

Eli was already out of the booth and tossing money on the table. "Where?" he asked, when she disconnected and slid out of the booth.

She looked up at him, her eyes full of worry. "The hospital."

CHAPTER THIRTEEN

"You rode a mechanical bull?"

Caitlyn had already asked her brother that question twice, but she was still waiting for him to say "just kidding" or "no, that would be stupid."

Bryan grinned at her. "Are you sure you're not the one with the concussion?" he asked. "Your hearing's not so good."

No, *he* was the one with the concussion. He was the one who had fallen and whacked his head. He was also the one who had undergone an x-ray and MRI for hip pain that hadn't been there before he'd gone into the Roadhouse.

"You rode a mechanical bull." She shook her head. "What were you thinking?"

"I was thinking that I've never ridden a mechanical bull before and I really wanted to try it," Bryan said.

Caitlyn gripped the railing of her brother's bed. His *hospital* bed. Her brother was in the hospital. She'd taken him on a trip, one trip, and now he was in the hospital, away from his doctors. And doing stupid shit.

She should have known.

Bryan and Ty were the kings of the stupid shit club. They always had been. Along with their love for all things that would make their mothers have heart palpitations, they'd both been blessed with the tendency to always land on their feet.

The irony of that was not lost on her now.

"Bryan," she said calmly. "I realize we haven't really talked about all of this and I'm sure you don't want to think about the fact that you can't do all the things you used to do, but I kind of thought this was an obvious one."

"What was kind of an obvious one?"

"You spend thirty percent of your time in a wheelchair."

"Yes, that's about right."

She looked at him for several seconds, but he didn't go on. Okay. "I think that getting on a mechanical bull is a kind of stupid thing to do anyway, but I'm pretty sure that being in a wheelchair makes it an even stupider thing to do."

Bryan frowned, as if truly confused by that. "Why is that?"

"Because you could fall off," she said patiently, with the tone she used on the little kids who came into the Sweet Shop.

"People who don't spend any time in wheelchairs fall off of mechanical bulls all the time."

"Right. That's part of the 'stupid thing to do anyway.'"

"So why shouldn't I try it?"

"You could get hurt!" God, he was infuriating. She was happy to help him. Happy to be there for him. But he wasn't helping himself. "Your legs could not work the way they used to and you could fall off the damned thing and—"

"Caitlyn."

She took a deep breath and looked up. Bryan had been lounging against his pillows, looking like he was sunning himself at the beach. He'd flirted with every nurse who'd come into the room. He already had a side table filled with flowers, balloons and what she thought might be a pair of women's panties, but she hadn't looked closely enough.

Now he was sitting up, his usual cocky grin gone, a seriousness in his eyes that she hadn't seen since long before he'd been tossed down a mountainside and come up with a partial spinal cord injury.

"I did fall off the mechanical bull," he said. "After two seconds. But I didn't get *hurt* falling off the bull."

She crossed her arms. "Then how did you end up with a possible hip fracture and a concussion?"

"I went to the bar for another drink."

She raised an eyebrow. "And?"

"Without my chair."

She sighed. "Why without your chair?"

"Because I can do that," he said. "Usually."

"And tonight?"

"Going over wasn't so bad. There were tables and chairs between us and the bar and it was like twenty feet."

"But?"

"Coming back, with a drink in hand, was a little less steady, and then—" He stopped.

She narrowed her eyes. "What did you do?"

"Stopped to talk to...someone. My leg got tired, I didn't have anything to hang on to, and when I tried to take the next step I went down. I twisted my leg and whacked my head on a table on my way down."

Caitlyn winced but there was no need to go over how he should have known better.

"Was she blond or brunette?" she asked.

He grinned. "Brunette."

Wow, he really was...still Bryan.

Her heart ached as she looked at her older brother. Bryan had always been her rock. And if she was the one in the wheelchair, no matter how fine she seemed or wanted him to believe she was, he would have insisted on taking care of her.

Her eyes filled with tears.

"Hey." He pushed himself up even straighter. "I promise I flirt equally with all hair colors. I even bought a drink for one with purple hair."

Caitlyn started to respond but just then she heard the door open behind her.

"Mr. Murray."

Caitlyn turned to see Bryan's doctor coming through the door.

"Dr. Perkins," Bryan greeted.

"We have your x-ray and MRI results back." He

crossed to the bed and pulled an x-ray from the envelope he carried. He held the film up to the overhead light.

Caitlyn leaned in to see it as the doctor pointed.

"You have a femoral neck fracture. A hip fracture."

"Dammit," Bryan muttered.

The doctor nodded. "I'm sorry. But the good news is that it's a clean break. There's no damage to the vessels and nerves."

"Will he need a cast or something?" Caitlyn asked. That was not going to make getting around even easier. "Will he be able to use his crutches with it?"

The doctor shook his head. "There are really two treatment options for hip fracture. One is a pinning. We pin the bones back together and let them heal. There's no cast required but patients are non-weight bearing for six to eight weeks."

"No," Bryan said immediately, and firmly. "I'm not going non-weight bearing."

Dr. Perkins nodded. "I agree that's not the best option for you. I would suggest a total hip replacement. We'll put in a new hip joint, replacing the damaged area. You'll be able to bear weight immediately and it will be the least limiting."

"He'll be able to walk on it right away?" Caitlyn asked.

"Yes. It will be encouraged in fact. There are some risks," the doctor went on. "In addition to the usual things, you have a great fall risk. You'll have to be especially careful. If you fall on a new hip, you could dislocate it or fracture around it. You also have less muscle strength to start and obviously will only be able to progress to a certain point. It's important that you get as much back as you can to help make the joint stable."

Bryan nodded. "Not a problem. I'll work my ass off."

"I'll call the orthopedic surgeon in then for a consult," Dr. Perkins said.

"Wait, you're going to do the surgery *here*?" Caitlyn

asked. "Shouldn't we take him home?"

"We don't do these surgeries here in Kilby," Dr. Perkins said. "We'll transport him to Houston."

"But—" She looked at Bryan. "Do you want to stay here?"

"I'd rather go home," Bryan said with a sigh. "Damn, my PT is going to give me shit for this."

"God. I'm going to have to call Mom," Caitlyn said as the thought occurred.

In fact, she was a horrible daughter for not having called her mother already.

Dammit.

Bryan was in the hospital and now facing surgery and she was the one who was going to have to break it to their mother.

"She's going to freak out," Caitlyn said, rubbing the middle of her forehead where a massive headache was brewing.

"Don't call her," Bryan said with a frown.

Caitlyn dropped her hand. "*What*?"

"We'll get home and tell her about it then. It will better when she can see for herself that I'm okay. This is not a phone call she'll handle well."

That was an understatement.

Fatigue crashed into her suddenly. She couldn't explain it. One minute she was standing strong, making plans, and now she could barely stay on her feet. It was too much... Bryan and his wheelchair and his injury. Eli and Kilby and them wanting her to come and bake two weeks a month and sell her stuff here.

Eli. And Kilby. And baking.

She'd been having sex and eating ice cream, foolishly dreaming of what it was going to be like to date Eli long distance and then actually listening when he was telling her that she could have it all.

But it was never going to work.

She couldn't be here two weeks of every month. That was ridiculous. She couldn't afford to fly down here all the time and the drive, by herself, was crazy. And two weeks at a time? Really? Even before Bryan's new injury that would have been a long time to impose on friends and neighbors, or a lot of money to pay a professional to come help Bryan. And every month? They didn't have the budget for that.

And what about the two weeks she wasn't here?

Eli was just starting his career. He couldn't afford to be distracted by a long-distance relationship. He needed to be on, all in, completely focused. Neither of them would mean for their relationship to be a distraction, but how could it not be?

"It's up to you," Dr. Perkins said to Bryan. "They'll take good care of you in Houston, but if you want to go home, we understand. We can try to make the trip as comfortable as possible. But I'll warn you, it won't be easy."

"That's how we like it, right Bry?" Ty said as he strolled into the room with two coffee cups. He gestured with his elbow toward Eli, who was right on his heels with a cardboard tray with more cups, stirrers and sugar packets. "I found Eli going out of his mind in the lobby. Took pity on the poor guy."

"Hey dude. Thanks for being here." Bryan accepted a cup of coffee, then exchanged fist bumps with Eli. Eli distributed the rest of the cups while Caitlyn blinked back tears.

Was it just an hour ago that she and Eli had been kissing at Scoop? That he'd said, "we have forever now"? In that short amount of time, everything had changed. He looked so big and solid and like everything she'd ever wanted. She wanted to rush to him and bury herself deep in his arms, pretend none of this had ever happened.

But that would be a fantasy-land move, and someone had to face reality.

"Bryan needs surgery," she told Eli, keeping a safe distance from him. "He needs to get back home."

Eli nodded, clearly not hearing all the other things she was trying to communicate between the lines. *I have to go with him. This will never work. I can't go back and forth. We have to end this now. I'm so sorry.*

"Can we talk about hiring an ambulance service to get him home?" Ty asked the doctor.

"Over that distance?" Dr. Perkins asked. "Possibly. It will take some time. And money."

"We've got both," Ty said.

Dr. Perkins told them he'd make some calls and be back with news soon.

Eli, Ty and Bryan huddled together, making plans, completely leaving Caitlyn out of the conversation.

"Hey," she finally said. "What about me?"

Eli looked over his shoulder at her, suddenly wary.

"We got this," Ty said. "Word is you have some big plans in the works."

"What are you talking about? Where did you hear that?"

"One of the nurses was talking to Eli when we got the coffee. She's friends with Donna McIntyre who works with the Catfish. The team's all excited that you might be working with Scoop. Something about bacon."

"*What*?" Caitlyn stared at him. "Seriously?"

"That's what she said. Not true? The bacon part did seem strange." Ty asked.

"It's not that, it's just… Nothing's for sure yet." Caitlyn could feel Eli watching her. "The ice cream shop owner is interested in my Cracker Jacks and some other things. Bacon cupcakes. But we haven't worked out the details yet."

Under Eli's searching look, her face was turning a million shades of red.

Ty glanced between the two of them. "Ah, got it. Well,

that's cool. Your Cracker Jacks are amazing."

She gave him a smile she hoped looked genuine. "Thanks. Now can we get back to the main topic here? Bryan needs to get home."

"I'm going to go see about that ambulance," Ty said.

"No. No ambulance," Bryan said. "Jesus. My mother would have a heart attack if we show up in Sapphire Falls in an ambulance."

"Well, I really think you're going to hate everyone by about an hour in if we just put you in the backseat," Ty said.

"They can just give me something to knock me out," Bryan said. "And maybe one of the nurses wants to come on a road trip to take care of me." He grinned at the two other guys.

Eli laughed, but Ty nodded as if it was the most logical thing in the world. "I'll go talk to them."

"You're not serious," Caitlyn said, though she knew even as she said it that they were.

"We take her with us to make sure he's okay on the trip home, then put her on a plane back to Kilby. She gets paid for her time, to see the sights between here and Sapphire Falls, and time with us. She's coming out way ahead here," Ty said. "Eli, help me out here."

"He's making some solid points, Caitlyn." Eli grinned, and for a moment Caitlyn imagined him in the back seat with the nurse. Flirting. Smiling. Laughing. Not that it would be her business, not after she went back to Sapphire Falls.

The thought hurt too much to dwell on. She rolled her eyes. "You're not inviting a nurse along on the trip back. We'll get him some good drugs and we'll drive fast."

Ty shook his head. "Caity, you really need to learn how to have more fun. Grab opportunities. Say what the hell?" Ty headed out of the room, no doubt to scout for cute nurses who were able to just pick up and go tonight.

"Ty, hold up. I have another idea." Eli sent Caitlyn a quick, scorching glance then strode after Ty. "I'll be right back."

Caitlyn turned back to Bryan. *Have more fun, grab opportunities and say what the hell?* She'd just done that with Eli. Her one shot at the brass ring—and now it was over.

Her brother needed her.

And her mother needed her.

"I have to call Mom," she said.

"Not yet. Please," Bryan said, resting his head back against his pillow and closing his eyes.

"Mom needs to know."

"What Mom needs to know if that I'm fine. Just…wait. Until we can tell her everything is okay."

Bryan took a deep breath and Caitlyn wondered if he was falling asleep.

"Bry—"

"Cait," he cut her off, opening his eyes and pinning her with a stern look. "That woman let me believe in Santa until I was ten. She let me think I had superpowers until I was eight and then let me believe I was going to become a Jedi Knight. She let me believe that the mustache I tried to grow in high school looked good. I'm going to let her believe everything is fine right now."

Caitlyn felt fatigue and frustration wash over her. She rubbed the middle of her forehead. "I don't get it."

"It's called hope, Cait," Bryan said quietly. "And it's the most important thing you can have."

"Okay, we're all set."

Caitlyn looked up to see Ty and Eli coming through the door with the charge nurse. She couldn't look directly at Eli because it hurt too much, so she addressed Ty.

"We have an ambulance?" Caitlyn asked.

"No need for an ambulance when you have a friend with a private plane," Ty said with a grin.

Bryan chuckled. "Levi?" Levi was Levi Spencer, the millionaire Vegas playboy who had come to Sapphire Falls for some R & R and had fallen in love with the town and with his new wife, Kate.

"You got it. It was Eli's idea. Hailey called him and he said of course," Ty said.

Eli shoved his hands in his pockets. "It's nice to have a millionaire in town."

"I've always wanted to ride in Levi's plane," Bryan said. "That's awesome."

Well, that took care of that. Far be it from Caitlyn to turn down that kind of help.

"I'll drive the car back," Ty said. "You two will get on the plane in about an hour."

"We are sending your tests and x-rays to Denver," the nurse added. "They'll coordinate the consults and scheduling up there. Everything will be ready to go when you get to the hospital."

Caitlyn felt a little lighter listening to the plans. They'd get Bryan home quickly, fix his hip and get him back on his feet—literally.

And her and Eli? Finally she met his eyes, saw the questions burning there. But what could she say? There was no Santa, Bryan was never going to be one hundred percent, and long-distance relationships never worked out.

Would it be better to let him keep hoping? Was hope the most important thing he could have? Or was it more cruel to let Eli continue to hope when it was hopeless? "Eli... I..." Her throat closed up tight. Both options were horrible. There was no good choice.

She saw the exact moment when he got it. When he knew she was leaving, and not just leaving for now. Leaving Kilby and their plans, leaving him, leaving *them*. He squared his shoulders, as if bracing for the blow.

She still couldn't speak, because if she did, she would either burst out crying or change her mind and throw herself into his arms.

But because Eli was Eli, because he was the best, the only man in the world for her, he spoke first. "Take care of him," he told her softly.

She nodded tightly. He attempted a smile, but failed miserably. The only man she'd ever loved bent to give her brother a quick hug, then left the room without looking at her again.

And Caitlyn had her answer. Hope or no hope, nothing could be worse than leaving Eli.

She'd rather get trampled by a mechanical bull.

CHAPTER FOURTEEN

Long, tedious road trips were an essential and detested part of the minor league lifestyle. Most guys jammed on the headphones, some played cards or games on their iPads. Trevor Stark seemed to be sleeping off a hangover behind sepia-toned aviator shades. Jim Bieberman was reading some kind of medical manual, and Shizuko, the hotshot Japanese right fielder, was updating his Instagram for the twentieth time that day.

Eli barely noticed the West Texas landscape sliding past the window of the Catfish bus. He kept reliving every moment of that last day with Caitlyn over and over again, trying to figure out what he could have done differently.

As soon as Ty had led him into Bryan's hospital room, he'd seen the end written all over Caitlyn's worried face. And even though he loved Bryan like a brother, he could have socked the idiot. Mechanical bull? What had Bry been thinking? Maybe Eli would have done something like that in his reckless high school days, but his father's stroke had knocked the stupid right out of him.

Or maybe not.

Did he do the stupidest thing of his life in that Kilby hospital room? Should he have made Caitlyn spell it out that she was breaking things off? Should he have begged her not to give up on them yet? Was he the world's biggest asshole for arranging a plane to fly the girl he loved a thousand miles away?

But he couldn't bear the misery on her face. He'd wanted to make it easy for her to do what she had to do.

He hadn't spoken to Caitlyn since then. She'd dropped him like a fumbled ground ball. He'd called her several times, only to get her voice mail. "You've reached Caitlyn Murray. I'm busy cooking up something sweet but I'll call you back as soon as I can."

Except she hadn't. He hadn't hallucinated the whole
thing about the Cracker Jacks at Scoop, had he? What
about that "I love you" she'd laid on him? Was it just a
heat-of-the-moment kind of thing?

His last words to her hadn't even been "goodbye" or "I
love you" or "you have a little bit of frosting left on your
hip."

No, they'd been "take care of him." World's biggest
idiot, right?

The thing was…

He knew Caitlyn. She always dropped everything when
someone needed her. Just look at how sweet she was with
his father. In the early days after Chip's stroke, she used to
come over and read the newspaper to him. Not just the
front page and the sports, but his favorite part—the boring
real estate section. As soon as Caitlyn's pretty voice started
reading off things like, "Five bedrooms, two baths, updated
kitchen…" the rest of the family knew they could relax for
a while.

When Bryan had his accident, Caitlyn had left her own
life in Denver to come help him. So what was she doing
now that her brother had suffered another injury?

Taking care of him. Of course she was. And Eli
couldn't argue with that. *Wouldn't* argue with that. He
knew exactly what that choice felt like.

"You all right over there?"

Eli looked over in surprise as Trevor Stark addressed
him from across the aisle. The star had taken off his shades,
revealing tired eyes.

"Fine," Eli said guardedly.

"I saw what happened with your friend."

"Yeah. Thanks. He's an idiot."

Trevor shrugged. "Guy's gotta do what a guy's gotta
do. Think that changes because he's in a wheelchair?"

"He wasn't in his wheelchair. That's the whole point.

He thinks he can do everything like before. He can't."

Trevor made another casual movement of his shoulders, which for some reason infuriated Eli. The golden boy, passing judgment on everyone else.

"What do you know about it, anyway? You've had everything easy. Walk up to the plate, get a hit. Walk out of the stadium, get a girl. You don't have any clue what regular people deal with, do you?"

The slugger's face took on an icy, stoic expression. "You don't know anything about me, Nebraska."

Well, that was true. "Same back at you. Which is why you should mind your own business."

"I intend to. Just wanted to say this." Eli longed for some headphones to block out Trevor's comments, whatever they were going to be. But when the left fielder spoke again, it was in a quiet, intense tone. "Things aren't always what they seem on the surface. From where I'm standing, you're the lucky one. Your friends came all the way from Nebraska to support you. You have a sweet little hometown backing you up. And your girl looks at you like you're an ice cream sundae covered in stardust."

Eli stared. Trevor had an "ice-man" reputation, but right now he read a whole lot of hidden pain on the man's face.

"You know what matters the most, Nebraska. Don't let it slip away. Fight for what you want right down to the last strike. Damn, I hate baseball analogies."

With that, Trevor slipped his shades back on, crossed his arms over his chest and turned his gaze back to the front of the bus. Conversation over.

All of Eli's anger drained away. For the first time, he'd gotten a real look behind the mask Trevor showed the world. Turned out there was a lot more going on with the guy than he'd thought.

Not that he agreed with everything Trevor said.

Lucky one? So lucky that when he'd finally gotten a taste of true sweetness, a taste of Caitlyn, it all vanished faster than cookies in the clubhouse? *Things aren't always what they seem.* Maybe Trevor was right about that one. Caitlyn wasn't skipping out on him. She was going home with her injured brother because Bryan needed her. He couldn't blame Caitlyn for choosing her family over whatever new thing was brewing between the two of them. What he loved the most about Caitlyn was her heart.

But it was exactly her heart that had pulled her back to Sapphire Falls. For good.

ﻬ

"Mom, this is not a good idea." Caitlyn tried to keep the irritation out of her voice—oh, how she tried—but it wasn't working at all. Her mother had decided that what Bryan needed above everything else was a backyard cookout, just like the ones he loved as a kid.

Caitlyn had loved their cookouts too, maybe partly because Eli had always been invited. Eli had taught her how to roast marshmallows to a charred crispy shell on the outside, gooey deliciousness inside. Eli had pounded the stakes on her little pup tent and held her hand when she cried because of Bryan's creepy axe murderer ghost story. All those memories made her mom's current obsession with hot dogs and s'mores particularly painful.

"Bryan needs to rest and heal. His surgery was only three days ago!"

"I know that, but he's always loved cookouts. I'm his mother and I know what he needs. He needs everything to be normal around him. That will keep his spirits up during this little setback. Remember when he broke his leg rollerblading on the roof?"

"You mean, *off* the roof. He went right over the edge."

"He's always been such a daredevil." Maggie Murray smiled affectionately at her son, who was sleeping on the couch, slack-mouthed, maybe even drooling a bit. Since the surgery he'd been taking a potent prescription painkiller that really knocked him out.

To be totally honest, Caitlyn had been tempted to filch a couple for herself.

"Mom—" Caitlyn ran through all the things she wanted to say. Yes, the hip will heal. Yes, it's a temporary setback. But he was never going to be "normal" again. Rollerblading off roofs was not something he'd be doing much in the future. And a cookout? Seriously?

Instead of giving voice to any of that, she let out a long sigh. "I'll go stock up on s'mores makings."

"None of that fancy Belgian chocolate of yours. Hershey's will be fine. That's what we always used to use."

"Yes, Mom." Geez, maybe they should all just hop in a time machine and fly back to the good old days of yore when the worst thing that happened was chicken pox.

"I'll go call Bryan's friends," her mother said happily.

And what, set up a play date? Caitlyn squashed the disloyal thought as her mom left the living room. She checked Bryan one more time, turning his head to make sure he wasn't going to choke on his own drool.

"Caitlyn," he said in the drifty voice the painkillers gave him. "Whazzup?"

"Oops, sorry, didn't mean to wake you."

He shook his head as if trying to clear it and struggled to sit up. "S'okay, sis. Ugh, legs like Gumby." The painkillers also made him talk like a third grader. "Gotta pee."

Caitlyn bit back a smile. If she were really mean, she'd take a few videos of Bryan on painkillers. She'd have blackmail material for years. "Okay. Let me help you up."

He gave an exaggerated frown as she crouched down to pull his arm around her shoulder. "Don't need help. Iron Man. Thor."

"Yeah, yeah, you're every single Avenger rolled into one. You can skate off buildings and leap mechanical bulls with a single bound. But right now, if I don't help you get to the bathroom you might pee on Mom's couch. And not even Captain America can get away with that."

He actually stuck his tongue out at her—darn, where was her camera?—but allowed her to assist him to his feet.

"Wheelchair, crutch, or shoulder?" she asked. Safest would be the wheelchair, but she didn't expect him to choose that. He never chose the safest option. His DNA didn't seem to allow it.

"Mom?"

"She's in the kitchen calling your entire tenth-grade class to invite them to a cookout."

Bryan squinted at her, as if not sure whether she was making that up. "Make her stop."

She nodded. "I'll try."

He swayed a little. "Chair," he finally said.

That one word sent shockwaves through her, but she hid her reaction as she helped him to the wheelchair, which was parked discreetly behind a lamp. Bryan must be really hurting if he willingly chose the chair.

Which meant he needed her.

Which meant she was exactly where she ought to be.

Which meant she had to stop tormenting herself with thoughts of Eli. It could never work between them. He needed to be right where he was, hurling knuckleballs on the mound at Catfish Stadium. She needed to be here, helping her only brother take a leak.

"Caitlyn, honey, I could use some help in here!" her mother called from the kitchen.

"Be right there, Mom!"

She got Bryan and his chair to the bathroom doorway, but he put his good foot down, stopping the forward motion before she could push him onto the pale-green linoleum that had been there for as long as Caitlyn could remember.

"I've got it from here."

"Bryan, you're woozy with the drugs."

"I've got it," he repeated firmly. He hoisted himself out of the chair and balanced with a hand on the bathroom cabinet to his right and the towel rack to his left. "I'm supposed to walk on it."

She knew that. She knew that the PTs in the hospital had gotten him up and out of bed and walking down the hall with a walker the same day as his surgery. She also knew little eighty-year-old ladies had their hips replaced all the time and walked unassisted within a few days. She'd seen them doing it. But none of them had an added weakness from a spinal cord injury on top of it.

Still, this was Bryan. Her brother. Her very independent, athletic brother. He wasn't going to let her take him to the toilet unless he was half dead. And then she was pretty sure he'd army crawl there in unbearable pain before he'd let her help him pee.

"Okay, your call," she said reluctantly. "Yell if you need me." She took three slow steps backward, waiting for him to come to his senses and ask her to help.

The last thing she saw was his gritted teeth in the mirror over the sink as he took his first cautious step.

"Idiot," she muttered under her breath.

But she would have felt the same way if she'd been there all the times he'd gone parasailing or launched himself over a crazy-steep bike ramp or climbed up the face of a mountain. So, this really wasn't all that new except that she had a front row seat for his stupidity now.

She headed into the kitchen, where her mother was staring at the inside of the fridge. "What's wrong, Mom?"

"We're completely out of relish. We can't roast hotdogs without relish."

"I'll add it to my shopping list," Caitlyn said gently. "Anything else?"

She couldn't see her mother's face, hidden as it was behind the open refrigerator door. But she thought her shoulders might be shaking. "Are you okay?"

The door swung closed and Maggie Murray turned to face her, a bright smile plastered to her face. Caitlyn knew that smile. It was the same one she wore when Dad left for one of his sales trips. The brave, 'we can handle this' smile. "Just fine, honey."

For a moment Caitlyn wanted to scream. *It's not fine! Stop lying to yourself!* But she remembered Bryan's words about hope. She couldn't take that hope away, because she didn't know what her mother would have left without it.

On the other hand, maybe she did know.

Having no hope basically sucked. It was a pit in her stomach and a lump in her throat and a general feeling of wrongness, like leaving the sugar out of a batch of caramels.

Eli must hate her by now. She'd left Kilby without saying so much as "thanks for the tour and for all the mind-blowing sex."

She was pretty much a human knuckleball.

With her mother busy compiling the rest of the shopping list, Caitlyn went back to the bathroom. Bryan was propped against the sink washing his hands. He looked a lot more alert now.

"No more painkillers," he told her.

She pushed the wheelchair through the doorway so it was closer. "Fine. Can I have them?"

He shook his head at her. "Am I that bad?"

"Oh God, no." She put her arms around him and rested her cheek against his back. "I didn't mean it that way.

"Mom driving you crazy?"

"She's okay. You know what I thought about just now in the kitchen?"

Bryan turned to face her, drying his hands on the extra-nice lace-edged guest towel Mom had put out for him. "What?"

"I remembered all the times Dad left her behind while he went off to convince hospitals to stock up on antacids or whatever. I used to watch from the living room when he left. She'd help him load up his samples and travel bag. She'd hand him his briefcase. He'd give her a nice long kiss, then bound into the car like he was super-excited to be off on his adventure. She'd watch the car until it went around the corner. Then she'd put her shoulders back and march into the kitchen. I'd race to get there before she did, in case she was sad. She always said the same thing, 'Well, there's only one thing to do when it's just me and you. What should we make this time?' And then we'd bake something. I really think that's why I got into confectionery."

"Because of Mom?"

"Because I saw how baking made her feel better. But just now I realized that she's spent her whole life putting on a happy face while Dad was gone. She had to, for us. That's just what you do, you know? You carry on like everything's normal. So your kids can have a happy, normal life."

A shadow fell over Bryan's face. He took the two steps to his chair, limping, but without any assistance, and eased into the chair. "I'm guessing this isn't exactly what she had in mind."

She wheeled him into the living room. "That's not what I mean, Bryan. What is normal, anyway? It means different things to different people. Like, what's normal for a teacher isn't normal for a…New York City cabdriver. What's normal for an accountant isn't normal for a…"

"Baseball player."

She stopped short, catching her foot on the pile of the carpet. "Sure. Baseball player. For example."

"Something happened with you and Eli, didn't it?"

"It's complicated." She hurried the chair the rest of the way to the couch, then offered her arm so he could brace himself while he transferred his weight to the cushions.

"He called me after the surgery."

Chills rippled through her. "That was nice of him."

"He asked how you were. As if he had no idea. You should have heard his voice. Poor guy is eating his heart out over you."

"What did you say?"

"The hell if I remember. Freaking painkillers."

She helped him swing his legs into position, then tucked a blanket around him. He lay back, exhausted by the effort of a trip to the bathroom. "Well, if you talk to him again, tell him I'm fine."

"Sure. Just like the rest of the family. We're all fine." He gave a tired laugh. "Maybe if you say it enough, it'll be true. Then again, maybe I should tell him you asked for a hit of my painkillers."

"Don't you dare." She held up his earbuds. "iPod or sleep?"

"Neither. Truth. What's going on, Cait? After Ty and I did all that hard matchmaking work, did you screw things up with Eli?"

"*What?* You did not."

"Sure did. Twice. Kansas City, then Kilby. Getting you two together took a lot of highway miles."

"You two idiots should mind your own business. I can handle my own love life." Caitlyn backed away before she did something stupid, like burst into tears. Because seriously, it was incredibly sweet that two guys' guys like Ty and Bryan would care about her romantic problems.

Former romantic problems.

After all, you couldn't have romantic problems without a romance. And she'd pretty much put an end to any chance of that.

"So let me get this straight," Bryan called after her. "You get to wait on me hand and foot, bake me goodies and help me take a piss, but I have to stay out of the mess you've made of your love life?"

"Yes," she managed. "That's right."

"Have you forgotten where we live? This is Sapphire Falls, sis. Good luck keeping anyone out of your business. Especially your quasi-paraplegic brother who has nothing better to do. And by the way, Eli is my friend. Have you forgotten that?"

Her eyes went wide as she stared at him in horror. Oh sweet lord. She *had* forgotten…well, not really…but for all intents and purposes. She'd been thinking of Eli as *hers*. Her dilemma. Her problem. Her mess. She hadn't thought about how her actions would affect Bryan.

"I'll…I'll call him."

"Yeah. You do that." Bryan grumpily settled himself deeper into the cushions of the couch. "Little sisters, I swear to God. You have to do everything for them."

Caitlyn bit her lip to hide her laughter, and hurried out of the room.

She had to call Eli. She had to explain the unexplainable. Hope he'd forgive the unforgiveable. All without getting her own heart ripped apart just by the sound of his voice. How was she going to pull this off?

∽∾

When Caitlyn's number flashed on Eli's phone, he thought his heart might drop right through his stomach. The team was in Reno getting ready to play the Aces. They'd completed batting practice and were due out on the field for the National Anthem in about five minutes. But there was no way he was going to wait for an entire game before hearing her voice.

"Hi Eli." Her light, slightly husky voice brought back a rush of memories. The moans she made right before she came. Her laughter as she teased him on the drive to Kansas City. The sweetness of her "I love you" in the booth at *Scoop*.

"Hi Caitlyn."

"I…um…I'm sorry I haven't…" She stammered.

He went cold. Nothing in her voice indicated good news or happiness about talking to him. She sounded sad and regretful, and like she'd rather be doing anything else than calling him. He cut her off. "How's Bryan?"

"He's a lot less fun now that he stopped taking the painkillers. So much YouTube material, you can't even imagine."

He laughed, although it took everything in him to sound normal. "Remember when he got his wisdom teeth out and spent the rest of the day saying how much he loved us?" The word "love" felt like a punch in the teeth, so he hurried onwards. "He kept saying 'Sapphire Falls forever' over and over again, remember that?"

"Yup, that's my tough guy brother."

"Must be a good sign that he went off the drugs."

"Yes, I think so. Either that or he was worried about pictures of his slobber ending up on Facebook."

He forced a laugh. Honestly, he had no idea he was such a good actor. "Gotta go, Cait. Everyone's heading onto the field."

"Are you starting?"

"Nope, I pitched yesterday. Third consecutive win."

"That's so great, Eli!" Her enthusiasm felt like a sword slicing him open. For a short time, he'd thought she was with him. Body and soul, heart and mind. Now she was…well, what she'd always been. A friend. Cheerleader. Candy-girl.

"Bye, Caitlyn."

"Bye, Eli."

He ended the call and viciously tossed his phone into his gear bag. He finished putting on his cleats and jogged down the tunnel that led to the dugout. The chatter of the crowd mingled with the hollow tones of the organ, the calls of vendors selling peanuts, the lively voice of Donna MacIntyre working the crowd.

He loved this baseball life. Every moment felt like a bonus, something he never thought he'd experience.

He barely made it onto the field for the National Anthem. As he stepped back into the dugout, Duke Ellington, the manager, caught his eye. He was a barrel-chested former catcher who'd been bouncing around baseball since the '80s. Eli stepped over to join him near the big fan that was stirring the overheated air around the dugout. The whir of the blades kept him from being overheard.

"Want you to know, the Friars front office is impressed. Solo gave them a good report. I've been telling them the same thing, but they like hearing from their players too."

"Thank you," Eli answered, trying to hold back the huge grin that threatened to take over his face.

"You can smile, kid. It's allowed."

Obediently, he smiled. He usually tried to maintain a stoic expression in the stadium, even when he wasn't pitching. He figured the less emotion he showed, the harder to read he'd be. It seemed to be working.

"I think you're ready for the Show, but you tell me. Are you ready?"

"I'm ready." Because that's what you said when a manager asked that question. No hesitation.

Duke squinted at the field, where Jim Lieberman, batting leadoff, was stepping into the batter's box. "You seem like a humble guy. Hard worker. What they call a lunch pail player."

Geez, that didn't sound very exciting. "Okay."

"We need more of that these days. In my time, guys like you were the heart of the team. They came in, got the job done, and went home. There wasn't all this Instabooking and Twitting and Slap-chatting and so forth. Did you know an umpire kicked a rookie pitcher off the field for bringing one of them selfie sticks on the mound?" He shook his head. "You're more of a nuts and bolts guy."

Literally. Eli allowed himself another small smile. "I did run a hardware store back in Nebraska."

"Well, there you go. Major League Baseball's ready for someone like you. Heartland, small town, good looking. Single?"

Eli considered that for a moment. A week ago, he would have considered himself off the market. Today? Well, his heart was spoken for, but… "I'm not married."

"No girlfriend stashed in your apartment? What about the bacon girl?"

"She's…uh…gone."

"The press is going to eat you up like cotton candy." Duke slapped a hand on his shoulder. "Keep up the good work. Wish I had ten like you."

"Okay. Thanks, Duke."

He sat down at the rookie end of the bench. Normally he would sit with the pitchers in the bullpen, but after pitching a complete game yesterday, there was no chance he'd get into the game today. He caught a couple curious looks from the other guys, but ignored them.

Was he really going to get called up to San Diego? This whole thing was like some kind of crazy fantasy, like pretending you're pitching the ninth inning of the World Series when you're actually pitching to a lawn chair in the backyard. If he got called up…for a moment, he let the incredible excitement of that thought flood through him. Friar Stadium. Downtown San Diego. Forty thousand fans. Gigantic Jumbotrons showing his photo. Clint Black singing the National Anthem. Holy crap.

Not only that, but…

He sat up straight. If he got called up, his life would change completely. When he went back to Sapphire Falls, he'd no longer be Eli Anderson, hardware store clerk. He'd be Eli Anderson, pitcher for the freaking San Diego Friars. The entire town would celebrate with him. He'd get free drinks at the Come Again for the rest of all time. They'd probably throw a parade, name a sundae after him at the Spot. He'd be treated like a conquering hero.

He wouldn't have a free second to think about Caitlyn.

The more he thought about it, the more a call-up to San Diego sounded like the answer to all his problems. All he had to do was pitch his ass off during his next couple of starts.

Dwight Conner, the center fielder, jogged back to the dugout after striking out. He muttered very unflattering things to himself as he threw himself on the bench.

"You'll get 'em next time," Eli said.

"I hate slumps," the center fielder said gloomily. "I hit better back in T-ball."

Dwight was actually talking to him like an equal, as if he might have some kind of advice to offer. "It'll work out. Slumps never last."

"I think I got performance anxiety. I need some Viagra for my bat," he joked darkly, making his bat rise into the air. "Luckily, the other one makes up for it."

Eli laughed, because even though Dwight's joke was lame, he felt for the guy. "Just don't stress about it. No point in that."

"Wise words, Nebraska. I'll keep that in mind while I go six games without a hit."

Eli was quiet for a moment as he watched the next batter, Sonny Barnes, hit a long fly ball to right field. "We're all pretty lucky, if you think about it."

Dwight was busy whispering encouragement to his bat and didn't answer.

For the first time, it occurred to him that his time in the hardware store, when he'd given up on the idea of baseball for good, might have helped his game. Made him appreciate just how incredible it was to be sitting in this dugout, with the San Diego Friars considering him for their roster. It was everything he'd ever dreamed of as a baseball-crazy kid back in Sapphire Falls.

And yet…that hollow feeling still sat in his gut like a lump of raw cookie dough. It had taken him so long to see that Caitlyn was the perfect girl for him. But it had taken no time at all for her to disappear.

CHAPTER FIFTEEN

Of course she'd broken the candy thermometer at Scott's Sweets. Because why should any part of her life work out?

Stop feeling sorry for yourself, Caitlyn lectured as she rode her bike toward Anderson's Hardware. Because of course the only store in town that carried her preferred brand of candy thermometer would be Eli's.

Because that's the way Eli was. He remembered stuff like that. Like what kind of thermometer she liked, and the fact that she loved having her nipples licked, and the way just lowering his voice to a deeper range could make the clothes practically drop off her body.

Eli had a very good memory. A very good...lots of things.

She rested her bike against the brick wall of the hardware store. That was one thing she loved about Sapphire Falls. Her bike would be safe here. No one would steal it, because everyone knew that only Caitlyn Murray had a little pink basket on a high-performance mountain bike. Bryan had laughed his ass off when he'd seen how she was using the bike he'd given her.

Pushing open the front door, she listened to the familiar chime of the bells. Before Eli had left, that sound had meant the next thing she'd see would be his handsome face behind the counter. He'd offer her that wide smile, his blue eyes gleaming against the backdrop of the display of double A batteries behind him. Anticipation would flutter through her as if the Fourth of July parade was about to start.

"Well, if it isn't Caitlyn Murray," Chip greeted her. "How's that brother of yours doing?"

"He's better. He got lucky that it's a clean fracture. He's going crazy lying around inside, but you know Bryan.

How's…" she hesitated. "How's Eli doing?"

Did Chip know that things had shifted between her and Eli? She hadn't said anything to anyone, but Eli might have mentioned something to his dad.

Chip's face lit up at the mention of his son. "He's knocking their socks off down there. He's got an ERA of 3.09 over seven starts, with three home runs given up and twenty strikeouts. No one knows what to do with that knuckleball of his." He rustled the papers clogging the counter and extracted a newspaper. The *Kilby Press-Herald*. "Know what they're calling him down there? Eel Anderson. Get it, instead of Eli? That's because he's so good at slipping out of a tough spot. The Eel." He chuckled. "Can't wait to rag on him about that."

Eli had slipped out of *her* grasp, that was for sure. "Did you subscribe to the Kilby newspaper?"

"Yup," he said proudly. "Gotta keep track of my boy."

She gave him her usual once-over. "I have to say, you look great, Mr. Anderson. I guess working the counter agrees with you."

"You know what agrees with me? Having my son do what he was meant to do. Nothing against hardware, it's been good to our family. But Eli's put enough time in here. I didn't even know it, but the guilt was getting to me. It's like a monkey off my back. So, Miss Caitlyn Murray, what can I do for you this fine day?"

Wow. She seriously hadn't seen Chip Anderson this chipper since before his stroke. "Well, I dropped a baking stone on my favorite candy thermometer. Eli usually keeps a couple in stock. Aisle Three. I'll just go check, okay?"

"You do that. I'm sure you know right where they are." He gave her a lopsided smile, since one side of his face no longer responded to nerve impulses. "I've got some box scores to check. Might take a peek at the real estate down there while I'm at it."

She smiled back as best she could, even though she had

a feeling that her smile was even stiffer than Mr. Anderson's. Real estate in Kilby—that brought to mind the happy picture she'd nearly experienced. Her and Eli, cozy as two peas in an apartment of their own.

She shoved the thought aside as she scanned Aisle Three in search of her candy thermometers. When she finally spotted the familiar blue box, a flash of yellow paper caught her eye. A Post-it was stuck to the top of the box. She took it down and peered at the words written there in Eli's jagged handwriting.

"Break another thermometer, Candy-girl? No worries, I got you covered. This one's on the house. You can pay me back with something extra sweet."

Tremors raced up and down her spine. Eli must have left this note before he left Sapphire Falls for Kilby. He'd been thinking about her during his whirlwind departure, when he was packing and saying goodbye and wrapping things up at the hardware store. Eli was so…amazing. Caring. Incredible.

And she'd left him in Kilby without so much as a real explanation.

She took the candy thermometer to the counter, where Chip waved her off. "Bring me some peanut butter fudge next time you come by. That should square us up for a while."

"Thanks, that's really nice of you. I'll make a batch in the next couple of days." Chip's attention returned to the real estate section while she headed for her bike. Her phone rang as she was swinging her leg over the seat.

"Hey, it's Peyton."

Caitlyn grinned. Peyton Wells was younger than Caitlyn by a few years, but Peyton worked part time at the Sweet Shop and they'd gotten to know each other better over the past few months. Peyton also loved to go out. A lot. She was a ton of fun. If you wanted to get up bright and early in the morning and be super productive and not need ibuprofen and gallons of caffeine to get through your day, then Peyton was not the girl to hang out with. But if you wanted to have a good time, laugh and dance and generally forget your troubles for a few hours, then she was your girl.

"We haven't had a chance to hang out since you got back from Texas. How about we go to the Come Again tonight?" Peyton asked.

"Works for me." It *really* worked for her. Bryan wasn't working tonight so she didn't have to worry about big brother stuff either.

"How's seven?"

"See you there." Maybe this was just what she needed, she decided as she pedaled down Main Street. Something to distract her from thinking about Eli twenty-four seven. Not even refilling Bryan's ice packs took her mind off him. It was her own fault. And Jägermeister's. She should never have ordered those shots, never challenged Eli to leave them behind if he wanted to take her to bed. She should have known she'd fall completely, thoroughly in love with him.

Jägermeister had a lot to answer for.

The crowd at the Come Again greeted her and Peyton with their usual good spirits. Caitlyn had to fake her smile, but even a fake smile felt better than crying in her pillow the way she kind of wanted to. Peyton forged a path through the mob, Caitlyn following at her heels. She cupped her hands around her mouth to shout her order to Derek, the bartender. "Two vanilla vodkas on the rocks."

"Is that Caitlyn with you? Tell her I have something for her," he answered.

Peyton gave her a puzzled look, but Caitlyn just shrugged. She had no clue what Derek was talking about, but maybe she'd left something here the last time she came in. It had been a while, come to think of it. She hadn't had a chance to drop in since she'd gotten back from Kilby.

Peyton pushed her toward the bar. "Didn't I tell you he had a crush on you?" she whispered in Caitlyn's ear. "Smile at him nicely and I'll bet we'll be drinking on the house."

"I always smile nicely, with or without free drinks," Caitlyn protested.

"I'm just saying. If you're going to kick Eli to the curb, you might want to consider Mr. Best-Cosmo-Maker-in-Town. He's hot, and I heard he knows his way around a Screaming Orgasm too."

"You shush," Caitlyn ordered her friend. "I thought we were here for girl-time.

"What's more fun during girl-time than talking about boys?" Peyton flipped her hair over her shoulder.

"What's to talk about? You ready to tell me how you feel about a certain Sapphire Falls cop?" Caitlyn wasn't the only one who had seen sparks between Peyton and Scott Hansen. Make that *Officer* Scott Hansen.

"Oh, no. We're talking about *your* boy department," Peyton said, shaking her head emphatically.

But Caitlyn didn't miss the pink in Peyton's cheeks.

Peyton Wells never blushed.

"Well, my boy department is shut down. Lack of inventory," Caitlyn muttered.

Peyton was still laughing about that when she greeted the attractive man on the other side of the counter. "Hi, Derek. How's it going?"

"Hey ladies." He gave Caitlyn a smile. "I've been wondering when you'd show up here."

Tall, dark, with a killer dimple in his cheek, he should have at least made her stomach flip a little when he grinned at her.

But nothing happened.

"I've been looking forward to this moment for weeks," Derek said.

"Well, I…uh…I'm not sure what you mean." Was he

flirting with her? Was Peyton right that he had a crush? It didn't sound like it, exactly.

"What I mean is, *this*." From behind his back, like a rabbit from a hat, Derek pulled out two full shot glasses and plopped them on the bar in front of her. She took a whiff of the dark brown liquid. *Jägermeister.*

Peyton looked revolted. "Is that Jäger? Why are you giving her that stuff?" Peyton wasn't a girlie-drink girl by any means. She could down beer and tequila and just about anything else with the best of them. But she'd always detested Jägermeister. Apparently it went back to an unfortunate river party when she'd been about sixteen.

"Following orders. These two shots are courtesy of the newest pitching sensation hitting the sports news."

Caitlyn still didn't quite get it. "Eli sent these? Peyton, did you tell him we were coming here tonight?"

Peyton shook her head, looking just as confused as Caitlyn was.

"He stopped by before he left town," Derek explained. "Bought these and told me to surprise you when you first showed up in here. He said you'd get the message."

Caitlyn felt her face heat to bright telltale red. She'd never forget those two fateful shots of Jäger in Kansas City, or what had come afterwards.

She picked up one of the shot glasses. Eli sure had been busy before he left for Kilby. Apparently he'd planted little reminders all over town. It was both incredibly sweet and a little torturous.

"What message?" Peyton looked as if she was about to burst from curiosity. "A message from Eli? What's the story, Caitlyn?"

"I have a feeling it's a private message." Derek winked. "If you know what I mean." Someone signaled him from the other end of the bar. He rapped the surface of the bar next to the other shot glass. "Drink up. I want Eli to know I took care of my end of the job."

"I can't believe he did this," she told Peyton.

"Me neither. What was he thinking? He could have at least ordered something drinkable. Maybe a Sex on the Beach or a Bend Over Shirley."

"A *what?*"

"A Shirley Temple with raspberry vodka. They're pretty good, actually."

Caitlyn touched her tongue to the Jäger. That night in Kansas City had changed her life. She'd never look at Jägermeister the same way again. But just because she'd always think of Eli when she had a shot of Jager didn't mean she should avoid it forever, did it? If she was going to avoid everything that made her think of Eli, she'd have to stay away from baseball and blue eyes and her old yellow Ford and her own brother and…well, pink frosting and hotel beds.

Maybe all beds, just to be safe.

She'd never have a good night's sleep again.

She downed the shot, then offered the other to Peyton, who wrinkled her nose in disgust.

So Caitlyn drank the second shot.

"Oh, so it's going to be that kind of night, is it?" Peyton hugged an arm around her shoulders. "We'd better get a table. Come on."

కుడు

Luckily, Peyton was more than happy to keep pace with her. A few more Sapphire Falls women came and went, but the rest of the evening was a blur to Caitlyn. She did manage to send a few texts to Eli, however.

Okay, maybe more than a few. Now that she'd broken the ice and called him, it was impossible to keep her hands off her phone.

Jäger? R u kidding me?

Hahah. Got you.

You're going to pay for this.

Already did. Did you drink them both?

She looked around the bar, as if he might be spying on her from the corner. *How can you tell?*

I know you, Candy-girl. You're Jäger-texting.

That's idiculous. Ricidrus. Ricidulous. Damn autocorrect.

Don't blame autocorrect for your two shots.

No, I blame you. For the thermomter too. Thertomet… *Damn.*

You aren't driving, r u? Or biking?

Peyton's here. So's Derek. Million others. I know everyone here. It's Sapphire Falls. Don't worry.

A pause, then: *Derek?*

Was Eli jealous? It was hard to tell in a text. He definitely had nothing to be jealous of. And it would be mean to make him jealous over something that didn't exist. But the childish side of her kind of wanted to. After all, he was down there in Texas with all those tall, long-legged cowgirls. Girls loved baseball players. Especially handsome, blue-eyed tall ones with rock-hard abs and that little arrow of hair that pointed downtown, and big hands that knew just how to move across a girl's skin, and…

She reached across the table and took a long swallow of melted ice from the dregs of Peyton's drink. Peyton was chatting with a couple of people at the next table and didn't notice that her drink had just been used to keep Caitlyn from overheating. Amazing what a few texts with Eli could do to her core temperature.

Where r u right now? She changed the topic for her own sanity.

Bed.

Grrr. So much for sanity. Now she couldn't get rid of the image of Eli's long, strong body stretched out in a tangle of sheets. It was so hot down there in Texas. He probably wasn't wearing anything to bed. He was probably lying there totally naked, all sexy and muscular and delectable.

She lowered her forehead to the table and banged it repeatedly against the laminate surface. Maybe she could knock her attraction to Eli right out of her. Or maybe this would give her a concussion. A concussion would be better than this constant pull toward Eli.

"Stop that, you're freaking me out," ordered Peyton. "See? This is what comes from drinking Jäger."

"No. This is what comes from *not* drinking Jäger."

Peyton looked at her blankly.

"It was a challenge. If we drank the shots, we'd stay at the bar, friends like always. If we didn't drink the shots, we'd go back to the hotel and get naked. Did I do the wrong thing, P? Did I make the biggest mistake of my life?"

"I'm guessing you didn't drink the shots?"

Caitlyn nodded miserably.

"Well, you know how I feel about Jägermeister. And I've seen Eli Anderson in baseball pants. You made the right call." She winked. "In all respects."

"But things are such a mess now. And he's so perfect and I drove him away. Like, literally. I drove him to that tryout. Now he's so far away and even though I'm really happy for him and I know it's the best thing... I miss him so much." She ended with a hiccup that jolted her entire body.

"Of course you do, sweetie. Come on, it's going to be okay. You'll move on." Peyton wasn't always the most comforting of friends, but her heart was in the right place.

"No, that's the thing. I won't. I know myself. I'll never love anyone else the way I love Eli. I grew up with him. Even when I was in Denver and I dated other guys, he was always in the back of my mind. Then I came back and he was even more amazing than I remembered, and all of a sudden he was all I could think about. And then..." She sniffed.

"And then came the Jägermeister."

"Yes. And then came Kilby, and it was the best time I've ever had. I don't even mean the part between the sheets. I mean the talking, the driving around Kilby, being together, just him and me. I don't think we could ever have been alone like that here in Sapphire Falls, you know? Everyone always knows what you're up to here. It was like a honeymoon. It was perfect. Maybe that's the problem. Nothing perfect ever lasts."

She drained the last of Peyton's vanilla vodka. Peyton eyed the glass with a disgruntled expression. "Well my drink sure didn't, anyway."

Caitlyn giggled, then covered her mouth as another hiccup hit her. Then they were both laughing so hard tears came to the corners of her eyes.

Girl-time. Maybe it wasn't sheer bliss the way her time with Eli had been, but sometimes it was exactly what you needed.

CHAPTER SIXTEEN

And sometimes you needed a giant bottle of aspirin to survive the next morning. Caitlyn groaned as she rolled away from the sunshine blasting through the blinds on her window. Her mother seemed to be yelling at her from the bottom of a well.

"Honey, how about if I take Bryan to his physical therapy appointment this morning?"

"Wha...?"

"You go back to sleep. I put some water and aspirin next to your bed. We'll be back in two hours."

"No." She struggled to sit up, though her sheets dragged her back down like swamp grass. "My job. Why I'm here."

"I know you're here to help. But I've got it covered today. I'll take Bryan for an ice cream cone afterwards, just like I used to do after Little League games. It'll be like old times."

Bryan was going to kill her. But her head was swimming and there was no way she could drive without a big dose of coffee. "Is the coffee on?"

"Sure is, sweetie."

Her mother left, a whiff of baby powder wafting behind her.

Caitlyn closed her eyes and let her head sink back in her pillow. She could sleep in, why not? This was her day off from Scott's. And apparently Bryan didn't need her help today. She could just sleep a little longer, then get up and pour herself some coffee and maybe make a plan. A plan for the rest of her life. A plan for how to move on, the way Peyton had suggested. People moved on from heartbreak all the time. If other people could, so could she. All she needed was a little more sleep and a mug full of rich, aromatic, mouthwatering hazelnut coffee...mmmm, it

169

smelled so real…clouds of heavenly French roast teasing her senses.

Wait a second…that coffee smelled too good to be a dream. She opened her eyes and caught a glimpse of white steam rising over the edge of her favorite cornflower-blue glazed mug. Someone was waving it under her nose, the aroma utterly intoxicating.

"Wake up, sleepyhead." The warm, rumbling male voice had even more impact than the scent of coffee.

"*Eli?*" Wide awake now, she pushed herself into a sitting position. "What…when…why…"

He laughed, his eyes just as clear and blue as the mug he was still holding for her. "How about a few sips before we get into all that?"

Was her subconscious imagining this? Was she actually still asleep? She took the mug in both hands and took a long gulp, keeping her gaze fixed on him in case he turned out to be some hangover-induced hallucination. But he didn't disappear.

She let out a long sigh as the caffeine hit her bloodstream. A dash of cream, tons of sugar, a good-looking man serving her in bed—perfection. "Am I dreaming? Because this is kind of too good to be true."

He took the mug from her hand, set it on the bedside table, then offered her one arm, his hunter-green t-shirt stretching across his shoulders. "You're welcome to touch if you need proof."

She traced a finger along the ridge of muscle of his forearm. His skin was warm from the sun. She met his eyes, the pupils expanding at her touch. "What are you doing here? Oh my God. Did something bad happen? Did you get sent back home? I thought everything was going so well!"

"It is. It's going great. Actually, I got called up."

"Called up?" It took a moment for that to sink in. *"Called up?"* she screamed. "You're going to be a Friar?

Oh my god, Eli. That's amazing. Does your father know? Bryan? Ty?"

He shook his head. "You're the only one."

The way he said it, as if he meant something much different by those words, made her breath catch. "So…what are you doing here? Wasn't I just texting with you last night? You didn't mention this. Did you? Was I that Jägermeistered?"

"So it's a verb now. Good to know. And no, I didn't mention it. I wanted to tell you in person."

Something was off. This was all wrong. Or maybe she was still too hungover to take it in. She put her hand to her forehead and pushed a tangle of hair away from her eyes. Oh no…what she must look like right now! Her fingers brushed against something…was that a…pretzel bit? From when she'd banged her head on the table?

"Eli, this is not good. You were not supposed to show up here out of the blue when I haven't even had a shower. Or…or…" She looked down at herself. What in the world was she wearing? In all her fantasies about seeing Eli again, she'd never imagined that she'd be dressed in a faded old sweatshirt from sixth grade band camp. She'd grabbed it out of her drawer last night without even looking. "Oh God," she groaned, burying her face in her hands.

A gentle touch on her wrists made her peek through her fingers. Eli's lips were twitching, as if he was fighting hard not to laugh. "Candy-girl, you're beautiful to me. No matter what's on your body. Or about to come off your body."

He put his hands at the bottom of her shirt. She glanced at the door, which was shut tight.

"Don't worry," he told her. "We're alone in the house. All clear for at least another hour, according to Bryan." Firmly, he tugged her shirt over her head. She raised her arms so the embarrassing garment could vanish from her life. When it was gone, she crossed her arms over her chest.

"You can...uh...put that in the laundry. Or the trash. Out the window, whatever. An incinerator would come in handy."

Laughing, Eli tossed it toward the hamper in the corner of her room. "You shouldn't worry so much. You could be wearing a pizza box and you'd be gorgeous to me."

"That's because you're a guy and you love pizza."

"No, it's because I love *you*." He ran his hands down her bare arms, sending shivers cascading over her skin. When he reached the rounded flesh swelling over her crossed forearms, she drew in a gasp of pleasure. His finger slowly traced the dip of her cleavage, then found the edge of a nipple. Sensation jumped from the tip of her breast to a place deep inside.

"Eli," she breathed, her eyes closing halfway. "Are you really here?"

"I'm really here."

"I'm really glad."

"Really?" The uncertainty in his voice made her eyes fly open. "Because I wasn't completely sure, after—"

"That was wrong of me. I'm so sorry. I shouldn't have left like that. I just didn't think there was any way—"

"It's okay, Caitlyn. I get it."

"I'll always be glad to see you, Eli. Even if it's just on the ESPN highlight show." She brushed her lips against his, the slightest, lightest movement that somehow made everything seem right again. "I'm really, really, really happy to see you, and I really, really need..."

He flicked his thumbs against her nipples.

"A shower," she squeaked.

"Not a problem. I do some of my finest work in the shower." Without any more warning than that, he scooped her out of bed and carried her to the bathroom. She'd claimed the small upstairs bathroom for herself when she'd moved back to Sapphire Falls, and it was overflowing with all her favorite bath salts and body lotions.

Eli stopped in the middle of the room, surveyed the plethora of cosmetic products, and threw his head back with a Tarzan-like roar. "Nothing makes me feel more like a man than fruity bath gel and a loofah. Unless it's those baby powder poofy thingies."

She giggled helplessly as he deposited her in the shower. He stripped off all his clothes, flinging them recklessly onto the floor, until he stood stark naked before her.

"Come here, you crazy man."

"Crazy for *you*." He grinned as he stepped into the shower with her. Bracing one hand next to her head, he hovered his mouth over hers. "Ready?"

She closed her eyes, waiting for his kiss, heart pounding.

Instead, water cascaded onto her head. Cold water. She shrieked and gripped his shoulders.

"Better than coffee, right?"

"I hate you," she spluttered, water droplets bouncing off her closed eyelids.

He turned a faucet and the water got warmer. "Do you love me now?"

"Not quite."

When the water reached the perfect temperature, she finally relaxed her tight grasp on his broad shoulders. She let out a sigh as steam rose around them. Hands slicked across her body, spreading a delicious-smelling lather along the curve of her ribs, the swell of her ass. He must have found her favorite apricot kernel body butter bar.

"Love me now?" he murmured.

She held back the dreamy smile that threatened to take over her face. "You're definitely growing on me."

He nudged his erection against her as if to prove the truth of her words. "Clearly I have to work a little harder to win you over."

"Don't let me stop you." She let her hands fall to her

sides, offering her body to him. She kept her eyes closed, not only to keep the water out but because all her other senses had gone into overdrive. The murmur of water streaming down the tiles, the sweet, fruity fragrance of the soap, the luscious sensation of Eli's hands sliding between her legs…it all felt like a dream. When his warm tongue touched her clit, she slipped into an orgasm so quickly it shocked her. Like cruising down a water slide.

"That's it, baby," he murmured. She clutched his wet hair, gasping for breath. "You're so sweet, Caitlyn. I missed the taste of you. I missed how you feel in my arms. Nothing feels as good as you. Nothing."

Spent, she leaned against the wall of the shower.

"Turn around and I'll wash your back," he offered.

Obediently, she faced the wall and rested her forehead and hands on the cool tiles. Eli's hands on her back were absolute heaven, the perfect balance between soothing and scrubbing.

Until he stopped. She whimpered in complaint.

He pressed his front against her back, each long inch of his body making contact with hers. "You know what I want to hear," he whispered wickedly in her ear.

"Fine," she said breathlessly. "I love your back-scrubbing technique."

He slipped his hand to her front, between her legs. "Is that all?"

"Okay, and all the other stuff you do with your hands. And your mouth. Etcetera."

She felt the vibrations of his laughter all the way down her spine.

"Etcetera, huh? Is that what you call this?"

His thick erection pressed between her thighs. She widened her legs to allow him an easier passage inside. He pushed her lower back down slightly and then he was sliding inside, and oh God, nothing had ever felt this good. Not when she'd given up all thought of ever doing this again with him. He took one long, careful thrust, as if exploring just how deep he could take her.

A low moan was all she could manage. Her body clasped his cock tight, the tremors from her earlier orgasm still there, like embers waiting to be stirred again. And just like that, pleasure burst back to life, fiery-hot. He bent over her, driving deep and steady, so strong, so solid, so...Eli.

"I love you," she said in a strangled gasp as she came again. He followed right behind her, emptying himself with a long, rasping groan.

"God, Cait. So fucking good."

"I know," she whispered. "Every time. How can that be?"

They held each other tight while they recovered. The hot water sluiced over their skin, beating the tension out of their muscles. When she'd regained her balance, Caitlyn took her turn soaping Eli. It was sheer pleasure, an excuse to run her hands over those flat abs and long, muscled thighs. How amazing that this spectacular example of manhood had been walking around town all these years, stocking shelves and ringing up sales as if he was just an ordinary guy. He was the guy next door...and yet so much more.

"I'm definitely awake now," she told him. "But I'm still a little confused. I wake up. There's coffee, there's you, there's a shower, there's crazy-hot sex, and I'm not complaining, but...why are you here?"

He looked down at her, his eyes nearly silver in the steam filling the shower stall. "I told you I got called up."

"Yes, you mentioned that. Goodbye Kilby, hello San Diego. Right?"

"Right. Except." He hesitated, something momentous simmering behind the forced calm of his expression.

"Just tell me. I'm dying here."

"I said no."

"You... I'm sorry, *what? You lost me.*"

"I turned them down."

CHAPTER SEVENTEEN

"Is that some kind of baseball term I'm not familiar with?" Caitlyn asked. "Because it sounds like you said no, you didn't want to be called up."

Eli could feel the tension emanating from her. Considering a moment ago he'd had her nearly boneless against the wall of the shower, this was an abrupt change. But he'd been expecting it. Caitlyn loved him. He believed that. Which meant she would always want what was best for him even if it meant pain for herself.

She would want him to go to San Diego. Even though it meant being without him.

Well, that wasn't going to happen.

"I told Duke no. I'm not going to San Diego." He wanted to hold her so badly, but she was crossing her arms, her eyes narrowed, and he knew she was going to fight him. "I'm also leaving Kilby," he admitted. "I'm coming home."

Any other girl, in any other circumstance, would have squealed and jumped into his arms and they would have made celebratory love.

Caitlyn, on the other hand, narrowed her eyes farther and said, "No you're not."

He sighed and reached to shut off the shower. Then he pulled the curtain open and grabbed a towel from the rack. He wrapped it around her. Typically, he was all for having any and all conversations with Caitlyn buck naked. This one, though, seemed to be in need of covering. He couldn't get distracted by her curves and her sweet skin and her...

Yeah, he needed to focus so he could make her understand his decision.

And then agree with his decision.

And then say yes to the question he was going to ask her.

Caitlyn grabbed the ends of the towel and stepped from the shower. Eli draped another towel around his waist, gathered up his clothes and followed her out of the bathroom and down the hall to her bedroom.

"I am, actually," he said, picking up the conversation again as she crossed to her dresser.

"No, you're not." She jerked a drawer open and flung a pair of jeans on the bed. She slammed the drawer shut again, hard enough to make the bottles of perfume and body spray on top wobble. She yanked another open and grabbed a t-shirt, tossing it over her shoulder to land on the jeans. That drawer slammed shut harder than the first.

Eli winced and watched her treat the drawer that apparently held her panties and bras similarly.

She turned to face him. "Look, this is a grand romantic gesture and I appreciate it. I needed to see you. We needed to work out that things are okay between us. But we can't do this, Eli. We can't do long distance. It's too hard. It's too distracting for you. It's too...lonely for me." She made a disgusted face. "And that doesn't matter. How I feel doesn't matter. I know that. This isn't about me, but—"

"How in the *hell* is this not about you?" Eli asked over her rambling explanation. "This is about exactly two people, Cait. Me and *you*."

She was already shaking her head when he finished. "It's not. That's the whole thing! It's about Bryan and my mom too. And it's about your dad and your family."

Caitlyn Murray had fired his blood and made his heart pump in the past, but he never would have believed it could be in anger. "What are you talking about?"

"Your dad looks so good, Eli. He is *so* happy, so proud. You can't give up on baseball. *He* needs you to play, don't you see that?"

Eli wasn't sure what to say. He had gotten in late last night but he'd seen his dad that morning and Caitlyn was right. His dad did look good. Instead of saying anything, he dropped his towel and started to dress.

Wordlessly, she did the same.

When they were both covered, he faced her again. "I know why you came back and I know why you need to stay," he told her. "Of all the people in the whole world to get it, I do. One of the things I love best about you is your huge heart, the way you put other people first. I love how you put *me* first and pushed me to go after my dream. But Cait, I want to be your *partner*. I want to be beside you, not in front of you, with you pushing me from behind. I don't want you to put me first, before you. I want us to be together, in the same place at the same time. Literally and figuratively. Always."

She was pressing her lips together and Eli saw the shine of tears in her eyes. "That all *sounds* great, Eli. But I can't live with the idea that you gave up something so big for me."

He took a step closer. "I would give up anything for you. Baseball is big. I love it. It's always been a dream. But you... God, Caitlyn, you're like...a wish. Something I didn't even put into my consciousness enough to dream about. You're all of these things that I didn't even know I wanted. Until you came along."

A tear slipped down her cheek. "I can't let you do this."

He opened his mouth to argue but she went on quickly before he could.

"Because *you're* my wish come true too, Eli. One of the best things in my world is watching you live your dream."

"Marry me."

She opened her mouth. Then frowned. Then opened it again. Then frowned harder.

"Caitlyn," he said, gently but firmly. He needed her to hear him. "Marry me."

She stared at him, her eyes as big and round as he'd ever seen them.

"Be my partner, in every way. Make a life with me.

Baseball…it's been fun. It's been exciting. And it's been *part* of my life. But there is a lot more to my life and the years to come than my knuckleball. I want it all—a wife, a family, a house here in Sapphire Falls, sons to teach how to play baseball, daughters to teach how to outplay their brothers. I want to be here for my dad and my sister. I want to help you with Bryan. I want to hang out at the Come Again with the guys. This is a great life. I know that. I'm lucky. I don't want to ignore or forget that." He took another step closer to her. "Marry me."

Caitlyn didn't move or speak for several long seconds. Then her head started shaking back and forth. "No," she whispered.

Eli felt everything in him go cold.

"Not now. Not yet." She said those four words a little louder. She straightened her spine and pulled in a breath. "Go play baseball. In San Diego. And when it's over—for whatever reason, even if it's twenty years from now—come home and I'll be here."

The cold was quickly replaced by warmth. This woman was amazing. He wondered if he'd ever know how deep her ability to love and care about others really went. He knew, above all, he was definitely lucky to be one of the people she loved. Why him, out of all the men in the world who could have had her, why he got the chance to spend his life with her, he didn't know. But *this* was the Show. Not the Catfish, not the Friars, not the pitcher's mound in game seven in the World Series with two outs and a full count. *This* was the Show he wanted.

"You'd wait for me?" he asked her gruffly.

She nodded. "I won't ever love anyone else anyway," she said with a tiny almost-not-there smile. "And there is an off-season."

There sure was. But that didn't matter anymore. Eli was where he was supposed to be.

His heart swelled. She would wait for him. That was

amazing. Big. Huge. And mattered more than anything else
ever had.

ঙ৵৯

"Cait, I really—"

"Caitlyn! Eli! We're home!" Her mother's voice
interrupted what Eli had been about to say.

Caitlyn jumped slightly. She'd been so caught up in the
moment with Eli that she'd forgotten where they were.

Damn. They were kind of in the middle of something
here.

Then again, she should probably be glad for the
interruption. She couldn't say yes to Eli's proposal. But she
couldn't say no to it again. She wanted it *way* too much to
keep saying no.

But she couldn't say yes. He had to go to San Diego.

But she didn't want him to go to San Diego.

Yeah, she was glad for the interruption.

"She knows you're here too?" Caitlyn asked starting for
the door.

"Yes, she handed me the coffee cup and told me to
come on up."

"Oh boy." Caitlyn hurried through the door.

Eli was right behind her.

"Eli, please tell your family that you're all coming over
for dinner tonight," Maggie said as they walked into the
kitchen.

The countertop was strewn with grocery bags and she
was pulling jars and boxes from them, a whirlwind of
activity.

Oh yeah, something had happened.

"Well, that's very nice," Eli started.

"I insist," Maggie said. "I'm going to be baking and
cooking all day."

Caitlyn gave Eli a worried look. "You okay, Mom?"

Maggie didn't even glance at her. "Sure. I'm fine. Just have a lot to do."

"Okay. Well, let me know if you need me," Caitlyn said.

Her mom wasn't going to tell her what was wrong and she wasn't going to say that she needed anything.

But Caitlyn knew someone who *did* know what was going on.

She pivoted and headed for the living room.

Bryan was just maneuvering himself from his chair onto the couch.

"You're not supposed to be doing that by yourself," Caitlyn scolded him, rushing forward.

Bryan slumped onto the couch and sighed. Then frowned. "I'm fine."

Caitlyn stared at him.

God, she wanted that to be true. She would give anything for her brother to be fine. For her mother to be fine. If they were fine, she wouldn't be here right now. She'd be on a plane with Eli on their way to San Diego.

But she wasn't on a plane. She was standing in her mother's living room in Sapphire Falls watching her brother struggle to get onto the couch without help.

That was *not* fine.

"Fine." Caitlyn threw up her hands, the frustration bubbling up and over the mental levee she'd built to hold it back at moments just like this one. "Everyone in this house is always *fine*! Well, guess what? That's bullshit! It's not fine. Not all the time. None of us are fine all the time! And you both need to stop saying that!"

Bryan lifted his eyebrows and glanced at Eli, then back to Caitlyn. "What's going on with you?"

"I proposed and Caitlyn is *not* fine with that," Eli told him dryly.

Caitlyn whirled on him. "You're going to tell everyone you proposed?"

Eli shrugged, but he met her gaze directly so she knew he was absolutely not nonchalant about any of this. "*I* am beyond fine with it."

She gave an exasperated little growl. "You should go."

"I'm not going anywhere, Caitlyn."

She took a deep breath and let it out slowly, then softened her tone. "Eli, *please*. I can only deal with one thing at a time."

Eli narrowed his eyes, clearly very reluctant. But finally he sighed. "This isn't over."

"Yeah, I know." She did. What she didn't know was how she felt about it. She couldn't keep saying no to him. But she couldn't say yes either. She really just wanted to pretend that he'd never asked. That everything really was *fine*.

There were moments when she completely understood her mother. Denial was much easier than being surrounded by options that were all equally difficult.

A very stubborn look crossed Eli's face and she steeled herself for an argument, but finally he gave her a short nod. "I'll see you at dinner then. I guess we're all going to be here."

She growled softly at that too. Everyone was driving her crazy. Unable to deal with him—and not throw herself into his arms with an *of course I'll marry you!*—she turned away, dismissing him.

She felt him move in behind her and kiss her on the top of her head. "Love you."

Her heart melted at that, in spite of the fact that he was irritating her. She didn't quite smile, but she wanted to. She wondered if all romantic relationships were like that—heart-melting with a dash of irritating.

A moment later, she heard the front door open and close and she propped her hands on her hips and focused on her brother. "What happened at therapy?"

"Nothing."

"What do you mean 'nothing'?"

"I mean, nothing. Nothing unusual. It was therapy."

"So why is Mom in the kitchen baking and cooking for the rest of the day?" Caitlyn asked,.

Bryan sighed. "Because it was therapy. Nothing unusual."

Caitlyn moved to sit next to him on the couch, her expression gentling. "What does that *mean*, Bryan?"

"She wouldn't leave. I told her she should wait out in the waiting area but she wanted to be in the gym with me."

"Oh." Caitlyn hadn't even gone into the gym with him. She always stayed out in the waiting area with her iPhone and Kindle app.

"Yeah."

She was quiet for a moment. "Was it that bad?"

Bryan tipped his head back on the couch. "It was just…usual. But obviously they don't let me get away with doing things the easy way."

"So she watched you exercise and walk and transfer and stuff?" Caitlyn asked, starting to piece the picture together in her mind.

"Exactly. Therapy isn't about doing the easy stuff; they make me do the hard stuff. Over and over again."

Caitlyn watched his face. His eyes were shut and his jaw tense. She reached out and touched his arm. "Did you talk about it?"

He nodded. "She asked if it was always like that and I said yes. She asked if it was getting easier and I said yes. She asked if it was going to get back to normal and I said no."

Caitlyn squeezed his arm. "I'm sorry."

He rolled his head and opened his eyes. "Don't be. It was time."

"But the other day you said you didn't want to take her hope away."

He didn't say anything for a long moment, then he said,

"I can't sacrifice your hope for hers, Cait. This is real, this is my life and Mom needs to accept it. This *isn't* your life and you don't have to accept it."

She frowned and pulled her hand back. "What do you mean?"

"I mean, you're staying because you think I need you. I don't. I need you to be happy."

"You need someone, Bryan. And who else is it going to be?"

He frowned and sat up. "It's going to be *me*."

"Right. Except for the stuff that you can't do."

"Dammit, Caitlyn!" he exclaimed. "Stop. Stop making this seem like some big tragedy."

"How is this *not* some big tragedy?" she asked him, feeling the tears burning her eyes. "It's changed all of our lives—mine, Mom's, yours for sure. You can't do all the things you used to love—biking and hiking, racing, diving, dancing."

Bryan nodded. "It's changed our lives. But it didn't *stop* our lives. And it could have. I could have broken my neck on that mountain and died. I could have hit my head and died. I could have—"

"Okay," she interrupted. She knew that. She'd imagined all of those horrible things after that first phone call from Ty following the accident.

"But I didn't." He sat forward on the couch, propping his elbows on his thighs. "I'm still here, Cait," he said. "My body has changed and the adventures are changing. But I'm still here."

Caitlyn looked at her brother. Really looked at him. Not at his legs, not at the crutch that was lying on the floor by the couch, not at the wheelchair. But at *him*.

He was the same guy. His eyes still held that same humor and mischief they always had. He still had that spark that said he'd never met a test he didn't want to take.

But he'd never done it for the trophies or medals. He'd

let Ty take the spotlight. He'd been fine being second place, or not even on the podium at all. Where his best friend thrived on being the best, Bryan did it all…just to do it. Just because he loved it. He loved biking and diving and racing.

"I'm sorry it had to change," she said softly. "You were so active, you did so much, you had so much going on."

He nodded. "So slowing me down wasn't such a tragedy really."

She gave him a frown. "What?"

"I had a chance to do a lot. I saw amazing places, tried amazing things. I lived hard and big and loud for a while. Some people never get the chances I had and it has nothing to do with physical ability. I was lucky. I *am* lucky."

Caitlyn shook her head. "You amaze me. You're in a wheelchair part time and you feel lucky."

Bryan shrugged. "I was running out of new stuff to do. And now I don't even have to leave the house to have an adventure. Climbing stairs is a challenge. It'll be a while before I feel bored or like things are routine again."

Caitlyn couldn't help but give a little laugh at that. "Like I said, you amaze me."

"Have you ever known anything that I tried to do that I didn't figure out and get good at?" he asked.

She thought about it. "No, nothing comes to mind. Unless learning to be sensitive and romantic counts. I'm not sure you've figured that out."

He gave her a very familiar, full-of-himself grin. "I said was there anything I'd *tried* to do."

She laughed again. "Right. Then no, I would say you've always figured things out."

"Exactly. So leave me alone. Go with Eli. Live your life. Have *your* adventures. I'll figure all of this out."

She opened her mouth to argue, but then shut it without a word.

This was Bryan. Larger-than-life Bryan. He'd had a

setback in his conquer-the-world plan, but he was right, he'd always been good at the things he cared about.

Partying, dating gorgeous girls, getting his adrenaline rushes and living on the edge had been the things he cared about. But yeah, he'd been good at all of that.

And he'd be good at whatever was next.

"You're going to need *some* help," she said. "You can't deny that."

He nodded. "I am. I'm going to interview some home health workers. I'm going to talk to Ty. And…Mom will be there."

Caitlyn sighed. "You sure about that?"

"I'm sure that it will be an adjustment. But yes, I know she'll be there."

Caitlyn really wanted to believe it.

"And I'm the best person to help her understand all of this," he added. "Besides, it will be good practice."

That got Caitlyn's attention. "Practice?"

"There's a certain sweet brunette who's going to need to learn all about what's going on and that it's not going to change me or slow me down."

Caitlyn knew he was talking about Tessa Sheridan, a local girl who had been a friend and classmate of Bryan and Ty's. Tess had been a little bit of a nerd in school, but she was sweet and Bryan had always had a soft spot for her. They'd never dated, though Caitlyn had suspected that Tessa had harbored a little crush on Bryan. He'd actually been more like a big brother to her—he'd taught Tess to ice skate, he'd punched the first guy who'd broken her heart, and he'd ignored his own date and danced with Tessa at their freshman Homecoming dance after the guy he'd punched had left with his bloody nose. At least until Bryan had been escorted out by the principal for punching the guy.

Caitlyn narrowed her eyes. "Does this certain sweet brunette know what she's in for?"

"I don't think the sweet brunette has a clue," Bryan said.

His grin told her that he was looking forward to that challenge as well.

Caitlyn wondered if she should warn Tess.

"And don't even think about giving her a hint," Bryan told her. "Tess deserves to be swept off her feet."

Caitlyn lifted an eyebrow. "Wow, that's kind of romantic sounding."

Bryan laughed. "Told you I can get good at anything I care about."

Wow, sticking around Sapphire Falls to see Bryan turn into a romantic might be one definite bright side.

"I'm going to go help Mom." Caitlyn stretched to her feet. "If we're feeding Eli's family too, she might need another pair of hands."

"Cait."

She stopped and looked back at her brother. "Yeah?"

"Marry him."

She sighed. "It's not that easy."

"It is that easy. You say yes and you start your adventure. Sometimes the hardest part is taking the big breath and the first step."

"Bryan—" She sighed again. "He said no. I don't even know if the Friars will still take him."

"I don't think the Friars know anything yet."

Something about that made her heart thump. She frowned at him. "How do you know that?"

"Mom and I stopped at the hardware store this morning for a new baking pan for the potato casserole for tonight." He rolled his eyes.

"Mom needed *another* baking pan?" How much was she planning to make today?

"Told you. Therapy was rough on her."

Caitlyn nodded. Okay, she'd deal with that in a minute. "So I take it you talked to his dad?"

"Yeah. Chip said that some guy named Duke, the Catfish manager, was the one who told Eli that he was getting called up. He's the one Eli told no."

"But didn't Duke just tell the Friars?"

"I guess a guy who works with Crush Taylor, someone named Stewart, convinced Duke to hold off on notifying the Friars. He's trying to get Eli to change his mind."

"Oh my God. The Friars really don't know yet?"

"Chip said Stewart has been calling for Eli nonstop. Once Eli stopped answering his cell phone, Stewart found their home number and the number at the hardware store. Eli doesn't know, but Stewart and Chip have been talking. Chip told Stewart that Eli was going to propose to you."

Caitlyn felt her mouth drop open. "What? Chip knows?"

Bryan grinned at her. "Eli knows what he wants. He's going to tell everyone."

"And now Stewart knows." Caitlyn realized that probably meant all of the Catfish knew. Hell, all of *Kilby* probably knew.

"Yep. And he thinks it's great. Said something about how great you'll look with a California tan."

Caitlyn felt her heart soften and a smile lift her lips. She liked Stewart. "How much time do you think we have?"

"Well, Chip said to give him a couple of days to work on it. Stewart said twenty-four hours, that's the most he and Duke can stall."

Her mind raced at that. A million things seemed to need her attention at once. Most of all, however, was the thought that she needed to get ahold of Stewart. Right away.

She didn't have his number. She assumed Chip would, but she couldn't go to the hardware store or their house without risking running into Eli. And she knew the next time she saw him, he would want to talk about the proposal. And she knew that she couldn't keep saying no to him.

She wanted to marry him. Of course, she did. She wanted to be with him forever. She hadn't been lying when she said she'd wait for him. She'd never love anyone else now that she'd given her heart to Eli and she would enjoy every second of watching his baseball dreams come true. It would be hard to be away from him, but if that's the way it had to be, then she'd make it work.

She looked at her brother though and couldn't help the little bubble of hope she felt rise up. Maybe she didn't have to be apart from Eli. Bryan was…good. He really was.

But he was only half of the reason she was home. The other half was her mother.

CHAPTER EIGHTEEN

Caitlyn pulled in a fortifying breath. One thing at a time. First she had to be sure that Eli had a spot with the Friars. Which meant getting ahold of Stewart. How was she going to do that?

The answer came to her easily.

Jill.

Jill, who wanted to buy Caitlyn's Cracker Jacks and cupcakes, was Stewart's daughter. Caitlyn had Jill's number. On a napkin from Scoop.

Thinking about Scoop made her smile and feel sad at the same time. How could she miss a place she'd been *once* in her life?

Caitlyn shook her head. Scoop wasn't what she should be thinking about right now.

Except that she could easily look up the number for the ice cream shop and find Jill if she couldn't locate that napkin.

"I'm going to call Stewart," Caitlyn told Bryan. "Right now before any decisions are made. I'll assure him that Eli will be in San Diego by tomorrow."

"How are you going to get Eli to California?" Bryan asked.

That was a good question. She could break up with him.

Except there was no way she could really do that. She loved him. She could never hurt him, even if it was for his own good.

And he wouldn't believe it anyway. No one knew her the way Eli did. He'd see right through any attempt to convince him she didn't want him.

She needed a plan. She needed a convincing argument. She needed...

A sidekick.

Or a few sidekicks.

She grinned at Bryan. "I think I have a plan."

"You need some help with it?" Bryan asked, sitting up a little straighter, a gleam in his eye.

"Yeah, I might need *a lot* of help."

Bryan rubbed his hands together. "I'm in."

She laughed. "You don't even know what it is."

Bryan lifted an eyebrow. "Since when has that ever mattered?"

She grinned, love for her older brother filling her up. He was going to be okay. He was getting stronger. He had a lot of friends. He was a business owner. At the time he'd first mentioned buying the Come Again when Tex and Mary retired, Caitlyn had felt sad that he wouldn't be able to accomplish his huge plans of owning a business and making a normal life in Sapphire Falls. But she hadn't been fair to Bryan or his fighting spirit and his eternally optimistic outlook. She hadn't trusted him to know himself well enough to make that kind of plan.

At that moment, she determined to be more supportive. She was going to stop telling the people she loved about the things they couldn't do and start believing wholeheartedly that they could do anything they wanted.

That definitely included Eli. He could have it all. She could help him have it all.

Caitlyn felt her heart flip. There was still a chance for Eli in San Diego.

There was still a chance for *them* in San Diego.

Suddenly a loud crash sounded from the kitchen. A metal pan hitting the linoleum.

Caitlyn met Bryan's wide eyes.

"Uh, I'll be right back," she said, starting for the kitchen.

"I'll be right here," he said dryly.

She hesitated for a moment, then crossed back to the couch, leaned over and kissed his cheek. "You do amaze me," she said quietly.

He smiled. "If I had a nickel for every time a girl's said *that* to me."

Caitlyn rolled her eyes, but laughed. Yeah, he was going to be okay.

She hurried to the kitchen. Her mother had every cupboard open, the countertops covered with supplies and multiple pots and pans. Maggie Murray now knelt on the floor cleaning up blobs of what looked like brownie batter.

"Mom? Can I help?"

"Do you think lasagna and chicken casserole will be enough? I'll have garlic bread, lettuce salad, green beans, pasta salad, baked potatoes and fruit salad. I'll also have brownies and cheesecake. Or, I *was* going to have brownies." Maggie got to her feet and put the pan in the sink. "I don't know if I have enough sugar to make another batch."

Caitlyn stared at her. Okay, this was bad. She'd never seen her mom make *this* much food at once.

She moved in beside her. "What can I do?"

"Go next door and get some sugar from Mrs. Wright?"

Caitlyn nodded, then said carefully, "I'll ask Bryan to go."

Their father had, after all, built a brand-new ramp on the front of the house for Bryan's chair. And Bryan's upper-body strength was phenomenal. He could easily get the chair up and down the ramp and over the sidewalk by himself. Or he could probably even use his crutch.

It was as much Caitlyn's fault as anyone's that their mother didn't see that. Because Caitlyn hadn't seen it either.

Maggie sniffed. "Okay."

Slightly surprised, but pleased, Caitlyn called out the favor to Bryan.

"On it!" was his reply.

"Now what can I do in here?" Caitlyn asked.

Maggie directed her to the pasta salad prep and they

worked together for nearly twenty minutes without talking. Caitlyn also mixed the fruit salad and buttered the bread. She was in the middle of cutting tomatoes for the salad when Bryan rolled into the house with a small container of sugar.

He grinned. "Ask and ye shall receive."

Clearly the moment had been big for Bryan as well.

Maggie turned to look at him. For a moment, her lip trembled. Then she smiled, took the sugar and kissed him on the cheek. "Thanks, honey."

Bryan spun in his chair and headed for the living room.

Maggie watched him go. "He's not going to get better."

Caitlyn finished the tomato. "He *is* going to get better. He's gotten a lot better already."

"But he's not going to be back to normal."

Caitlyn put her knife down and turned to her mom. "He's the same guy he's always been, Mom. His legs just don't work the same way anymore."

Maggie took a shaky breath and nodded. "I know."

"It doesn't mean things are bad. They're just different." Caitlyn was happy to find that those words came easily and that she absolutely meant them.

Maggie nodded again. "It's just so hard to see your kids hurting."

"Of course it is." Caitlyn moved to put an arm around her. "But he's not hurting, Mom. I mean, yes, his hip is hurting right now at times and I'm sure therapy made that a little worse, but he's not hurting emotionally. And the physical pain is going to get better."

Maggie took a deep breath and looked at Caitlyn. "It's hard for me to see you hurting too."

Caitlyn pulled back, surprised. "I know I've seemed upset over Bryan, but I'm not really. Well, not anymore. I know he's going to be okay."

"Not Bryan, honey," Maggie said, turning fully and taking Caitlyn's hands. "Eli."

Caitlyn swallowed. Oh. "Eli." She didn't know what else to say.

A few hours ago, before she'd seen him again, made love to him, had him *propose* to her, before she'd realized that she'd been underestimating her brother, she would have said Eli was a friend, or that he had been a fling. But now...

Now it was time for the truth. For all of them.

She nodded. "I'm in love with Eli."

Maggie smiled, her expression softening. "I know you are."

"He asked me to marry him."

Maggie didn't seem shocked. "What did you say?"

Caitlyn shrugged. "I said no. He has a chance to go play ball in the big leagues."

"So Chip said," Maggie told her. "And that's wonderful. I don't understand what one has to do with the other."

Honesty. That was what they all needed.

But it was hard.

"When he asked, I didn't think I could leave Bryan. And you."

Maggie searched Caitlyn's eyes. Caitlyn wondered what she saw.

"But now something's changed?"

"Yes, Bryan..." Then Caitlyn realized that no, nothing had changed. Except Caitlyn's ability to see clearly what was right in front of her. She shook her head. "No. Not really. Except maybe my belief that dreams can actually come true."

Maggie took her by the shoulders. "Bryan and I are going to be okay," she said. "I'm going to talk to your father about cutting back on his travel. It's time he thinks about at least partial retirement. And Bryan told me today that he'd like to move out. He wants to have his own place."

Caitlyn was surprised. For two seconds. Then she nodded. "I think that would be good. After his hip heals."

Maggie smiled. "That's what I told him. But I also told him that I would still be cooking and putting food in his freezer and there wasn't anything he could do about it."

Caitlyn laughed and pulled Maggie in for a hug. "I'm so glad."

Maggie squeezed her and then let her go. "I am too. And now, let's talk about Eli and what you're going to do."

"What I'm going to do?"

"You're going to need to stock up on sunscreen. Your fair skin in California is a recipe for burns. And you'll need some California clothes. We could go shopping next week."

Caitlyn felt her heart swell. "Well, that sounds awesome. But I might need a raincheck on the shopping spree."

"Oh?"

"I have a plan. But I need your help. All of your help—Bryan and Chip and Stewart—everyone. And it has to happen tonight."

Maggie gave her a smile that made tears sting Caitlyn's eyes. She saw love and pride and happiness and even a little mischief in her mom's eyes.

"Then I'll just send you a couple of sundresses I saw downtown at Julie's that I thought you'd love and we'll shop when you come home to visit," Maggie said.

At that, a tear slipped down Caitlyn's cheek. "I would love that, Mom."

Maggie wiped the tear and gave her a smile. "Now get back to work. We're not just having company tonight; it's family coming over."

෧෨

Eli paced across the living room for the seventh time.

He wanted to get to Caitlyn. Yes, the dinner with their families was going to be nice, yes, he was glad to see his dad eager for the night out, yes, he was thrilled that this was the start of many family times all together.

But mostly he needed to see her. See how she was after talking with Bryan. See how she was dealing with her mom's obvious unhappiness.

See if she still thought getting married was a bad idea.

Because he was going to change her mind about *that*.

In fact, he was going to help her with all of it—Bryan, Maggie, and anything else that Caitlyn had going on in her life.

That's how it was going to be from now on.

She needed to start understanding that. Right now.

And she would if his father would quit fussing with his bow tie and get in the damned car already.

"Dad, you don't even have to wear a tie," Eli called. Chip was in the washroom just off the front foyer, peering into the mirror and undoing the tie for the twelfth time. At least.

"I want to look nice. This is a big night. Nothing wrong with a tie for dinner," Chip said.

Eli seriously thought he could count on one hand how many times he'd seen his father wear a tie of any kind. He hadn't even known his dad owned a *bow* tie. Who wore bow ties anymore?

"It's the Murrays, Dad," Eli said. "We've known them our entire lives. You don't have to impress them."

"They're going to be your in-laws," Chip said. "This is the first time we've all been together since you and Cait finally figured things out."

Eli stopped pacing and couldn't help but grin. "Finally?" he asked.

Chip rolled into the room in his wheelchair, a crisp, tightly tied bow tie at his neck.

"Finally," he confirmed. "What you were doing here all

that time and *not* taking her out, I'll never know."

Eli felt the same way. Now. He knew at the time, he'd had good reason to stay away from Caitlyn. Or he'd thought he had.

But that was in the past. There was no more staying away from Caitlyn. Ever.

"Yeah, okay. Let's go already."

"Lindsay!" Chip called. "You ready?"

"Um..." came Eli's sister's voice. "I think so?"

Eli frowned. That was a weird answer. "Are you ready to go to Caitlyn's or not?" he asked.

"Are *you* ready, Dad?" Lindsay asked from the top of the stairs.

"Yep! All ready!" Chip answered brightly.

"Okay, then I'm ready too." Lindsay descended the stairs. She wasn't quite bow-tie level dressed up but she looked very nice in a skirt and sandals with her hair curled.

For a second, Eli felt his heart squeeze. God, he was proud of her. And his dad. He loved them so much. He was so glad to be home.

You miss the mound. You miss the feel of the ball in your glove. You miss the smell of the peanuts and popcorn and the electricity of game day.

The voice that whispered through his head wasn't new. He'd been, of course, thinking about everything he was leaving behind to come back to Sapphire Falls. Of course there were things about baseball he'd miss. It was in his blood.

But family and love and home and *Caitlyn* were in his soul.

He couldn't have it *all*, but he could have what mattered most.

"Since when does Dad being ready to go affect whether you're ready or not?" Eli asked his sister as he pulled the front door open and ushered them through.

"Just... I was..." Lindsay stumbled.

"I told her to take her time because I was going to primp for a while myself tonight," Chip said, the motor on his chair whirring as he started for the ramp off the side of the porch.

Without any instruction, or seemingly any real conscious thought, Lindsay moved into place to descend in front of Chip on the ramp. It was a safety technique they'd been taught. It was a very slim chance, but it was possible that the chair could tip and if it did, obviously Chip would go downhill. So his caregivers had been taught to be downhill from him when he was on the ramp.

Eli watched as Lindsay helped Chip off the end of the ramp and stayed beside him as they went to the car. She assisted him into the passenger side and then stored the chair in the garage. While they were out, Chip used a manual chair that was easier to fold up and get in and out of the car.

Eli was still staring when Lindsay looked up at him. "You driving or me?" she asked.

"Uh..." He shook himself. His sister had stepped in without a single problem.

One more thing he and Caitlyn had in common—they underestimated the strength and compassion of the people in their lives.

"You drive," he told her, getting into the backseat and turning it all over to Lindsay for perhaps the first time in his life.

CHAPTER NINETEEN

Dinner was fun. It was loud and full of laughter, thanks in great part to the fact that Bryan and Chip had similar senses of humor. There was also *a lot* of food. Fortunately, Ty and Hailey had joined them, along with Levi and Kate—the Murrays' way of thanking Levi for the loan of his private plane—or the leftovers would have been even more ridiculous. As it was, Maggie had already promised to put together multiple containers for them to take home and freeze for future dinners.

Which wasn't all bad. Lindsay had stepped up in a number of ways and she wasn't a terrible cook. But there was a lot of distance between not-terrible and Maggie-Murray level cooking.

"Oh, darn it," Maggie said, coming back into the room with the brownies and cheesecake. "I didn't get ice cream when I was at the store."

"Oh, we don't need ice cream, Maggie," Eli assured her.

"Yes, we do."

Ty, Bryan and Levi all spoke at once and then shot each other looks.

Caitlyn narrowed her eyes at Bryan but then turned to her mother with a smile. "I can run and get some," she offered.

"Oh, that would be so nice," Maggie said. "Thank you."

Eli looked over at Lindsay. "Linds, you could go."

Caitlyn was clearly helping her mother hostess for the evening. There was no reason she had to be the one to run to the store in the middle of entertaining guests.

Lindsay looked from him to Caitlyn to Maggie to Chip and back to him. "Um."

Caitlyn slid her chair back quickly. "Don't be silly. I'll go. It's no problem."

200

"But—" he started.

"You should go with her," Chip said to Eli. "Keep her company."

It was four blocks to the store. But who was Eli to argue with a chance to be alone with Caitlyn? He'd kissed her when she'd first greeted them at the door but it had been a chaste hello kiss versus the hot, sweet, deep one he really wanted to lay on her.

"Absolutely. Great idea," Eli said, pushing his chair back and standing. Why hadn't he thought of it himself? They could make out for ten minutes easily. No, they wouldn't be able to blame their longer-than-necessary absence on traffic or road construction or anything, but he didn't think anyone here would actually wonder at all what had kept them. Or protest if their ice cream was a little soft by the time they got it home.

But just to be sure, they should probably make out before they got the ice cream.

Eli followed Caitlyn out to the car. He caught her wrist and pulled her around to face him, then backed her up against the driver's side door. He braced his hands on the top of the car, caging her in.

She smiled up at him. "Thought we were going for ice cream."

"There's something sweeter I need first." He leaned in and captured her lips.

Her soft sigh was exactly what he needed to deepen the kiss and press closer. Her body molded against his and after only a few seconds, the back of his shirt was bunched in her fists and she was up on tiptoe.

Eli didn't move his hands, or his body. Because if he did, this was going to end with Caitlyn naked in her mother's driveway.

She finally pulled back. "What were we going out to get again?"

She asked it with a smile that made him want to strip

her down as much as the kiss had.

"Lucky," he said. "We were going to get lucky. If we head up to Klein's Hill."

Klein's Hill was the main Sapphire Falls make-out spot. Everyone knew if a girl agreed to go up there with you, she really liked you.

"Aw, I've always wanted to go to Klein's Hill," she said with a small sigh.

He really wanted to take her... Then her words sank in. "Wait a second, you've never been to Klein's Hill?"

She shook her head. "Never kissed on the Ferris wheel either."

That was another serious romantic tradition in Sapphire Falls. It was the way to declare yourself to the girl you liked and let the rest of the guys in town know it was hands off. The progression went kissing on the Ferris wheel during the annual town festival, getting to second base on Klein's Hill, and then third base—or beyond—in the dark corners of the haunted house.

Everything in Eli wanted to do all of that with Caitlyn. Not because he wanted to get to third base—and beyond—but because she'd never done any of that. It was something every girl in Sapphire Falls should do.

And yet he was thrilled she hadn't done it with anyone else.

"It's beyond time for you to get lucky on Klein's Hill, beautiful," he said, reaching to open the door behind her.

"I agree," she said, surprising him. "And I'm driving."

"I can honestly say I've never been taken to Klein's Hill," he said, starting around the front of the car. Eagerly. More than eagerly.

"You've never been to Klein's Hill either?" Caitlyn asked, one foot in the car and one still on the driveway.

He looked at her over the car. "Oh, um, well...no, that's not..."

She lifted an eyebrow.

"I said I've never been *taken* to Klein's Hill. I always…drove," he finished weakly.

Caitlyn just stared at him for a long moment. Then she laughed. "Oh, um…well…yeah, I know."

He couldn't help but grin. "You do?"

"Eli, girls in Sapphire Falls have been talking about you for as long as I can remember."

"Oh." Yeah, he didn't really know how to respond to that.

"Are you feeling bad about your reputation suddenly?" she asked, actually seeming curious.

"I am just really happy that I get to be the first one to take *you* there."

"Little hypocritical, don't you think? That you don't feel bad about being up there so much yourself but you're glad I've never been?"

Eli thought about that. Yeah, it was hypocritical. And he didn't care. He was *damned* glad he was the first to take her up there. "Just get in the car, Candy-girl. This is gonna be a first for both of us."

He pulled his door open and got in.

She slid in behind the wheel and slammed her door shut. "Oh yeah?"

"Yep."

"How so?"

"I've *never* done the stuff I'm gonna do to you up there."

She laughed and put the car in reverse.

The drive to Klein's Hill should have taken six minutes.

Seven minutes later they weren't even going in the right direction.

He hadn't noticed because he'd been so distracted with the things he was going to do to and with Caitlyn on that hill. But when they drove past the park and swimming pool and past the huge billboard Ty had put up as a tribute to himself, Eli noticed.

"What's going on?"

"Just thought we could drive for a bit."

Eli looked over, saw the tiny curl at the corner of her mouth and it suddenly all became perfectly clear. They'd been in this situation before.

He settled back in his seat and draped one arm along the back of the seat and the other on the edge of the door. "Okay."

She glanced over. "Okay?"

"Yeah, I like to drive." He moved his hand from the seat to the back of Caitlyn's neck. He stroked his thumb up and down the side of her neck. "I like doing anything as long as you're with me."

She swallowed.

"And I hate doing things when you're not with me."

She looked over. Then back to the road. Then she sighed. "You know what I'm doing, right?"

"You're kidnapping me. Again," he added.

His chest filled with warmth and love. He didn't know what exactly this trip entailed, just like he didn't know what their life held in the future, but he *did* know that if Caitlyn was beside him, he'd go into it happily.

"I am."

"I certainly hope it's to Vegas."

"You've never been?'

"I've never been to Vegas to get married."

She glanced over sharply and Eli wondered if he should quit teasing her so she'd keep her eyes on the road.

"Um, so, no…it's not Vegas."

They were heading south. Which could mean a number of things. It could mean the airport or the interstate. Or, he supposed she could be taking him back to Kilby. Texas was south of Sapphire Falls. A long way south, but definitely south.

"We don't have to get married in Vegas," he said. "We can get married wherever we're going."

The skin of her neck was silky and warm and if he slid his hand forward he could feel her pulse thumping against his thumb. Hard and fast.

"You wouldn't want your family there?" she asked.

"That would be ideal. But if my fiancée is carrying out a surprise elopement, I'm not going to argue."

"I'm not officially your fiancée," she said, her voice a little scratchy.

She was choked up. He liked that.

"You are, Candy-girl," he said, turning slightly in his seat. "You're mine. In every way. Fiancée just means that we intend to get married. And we do intend to get married, right Cait?"

She ran her tongue over her lips, staring hard at the road in front of the car now.

"Cait? I need to hear it."

"Yes," she finally said softly. "Yes, we're going to get married."

Eli felt his chest deflate as the breath he hadn't even realized he'd been holding rushed out. He loved her, he believed that she loved him. But he really loved hearing the words.

"After."

He looked over at her. "After?" Had he missed a few other words?

"After the season's over. During your break."

The season. He should have known. "Cait, I already said no."

"You told Duke no. But he hasn't actually told the Friars yet. So you're still good, as long as you're at Friar Stadium tomorrow."

"How do you know all this?"

"Your dad said that Stewart had been calling. I got ahold of him and told him that I was going to get you to California."

He didn't say anything for a moment. Finally he

managed, "So the Friars…that's still an option?"

"Yes. Absolutely. They want you. And I'm taking you to them. To your dream."

His *dream* was sitting right next to him. Being kind of a pain in the ass. But his heart melted at how important this was to her. He smiled in spite of it all and wondered if that was what all romantic relationships were like—heart-melting with a dash of pain-in-the-ass.

Eli sat back in his seat. He turned his head, his thoughts whizzing as fast as the line of trees past his window.

The Friars. He could still go. He could still be in the big leagues. He could still have that dream.

Because of the woman beside him.

"I'm not doing it without you," he finally said. "I'm not. I don't care if you drive me all the way to California. You can dump me out there and I'll just come back. Like a dog lost from his home. Or one of those cats that gets separated from his family and then finds his way back. You can't get rid of me."

She laughed. "I'm not driving you all the way to California."

"Oh."

"I'm driving *us* to the airport. We're flying to California."

His head swung around and he took in her smile and let her words sink in. "Us? We?"

She looked over. "Us and we."

He pivoted on his seat as they passed the city limit sign for York, Nebraska.

"You're coming with me?"

"Of course. I spent all afternoon setting everything up. I talked to Stewart, I talked to Duke. I called Levi Spencer and asked to borrow his plane once more, I bought new sunscreen and sunglasses, and I talked to Lindsay about helping Bryan out."

"Lindsay?" he asked. "My sister Lindsay?"

"Yeah. She's such a sweetheart and she's got experience with being a caregiver to someone in a wheelchair and she wants to be a physical therapist."

Eli leaned in. "Lindsay wants to be a PT?"

Caitlyn nodded. "You didn't know? Because of your dad. She wants to help people recover after injuries and illnesses and get as much of their life back as they can. Bryan is going to have her take him to his therapy sessions so she can see it all firsthand and talk with the therapists and stuff."

Eli's heart was pounding. Everyone in his life was...going to be fine. Better than fine. Everyone was going to be great and it was because they all had each other.

He and Caitlyn didn't have to be the ones doing everything. The people they loved could take care of each other and love *them* enough to let them go to California for however long the league would have him.

And Caitlyn had made it all happen.

His hands itched with the urge to grab her and kiss her. The moment she pulled up at the York Municipal Airport, Eli slid across the seat, unbuckled her seat belt and pulled her into his lap.

He buried his face in her hair, pulling in a long breath and letting it all wash over him.

He was going to California to play baseball in the major leagues and Caitlyn was going to be there with him.

She squirmed in his lap, laughing lightly. She managed to pull back. "Kiss me already," she told him, taking his face in her hands.

So he did. Until she finally said, breathlessly, "We're going to miss our flight."

As they walked into the airport with their suitcases—his packed by his dad and sister—Eli had to shake his head.

"They were all in on it. Tonight before and during dinner," he said, just now realizing it.

Caitlyn grinned and nodded. "Yep. And they loved every minute of it."

Eli knew that having everyone else helping take care of him and Cait was going to take some getting used to, for both of them.

But he knew how amazing it felt to be there for the people he loved, and he was ready and able to let them feel that way too.

CHAPTER TWENTY

"Strike two!"

Eli breathed out and caught the ball Mike Solo threw back.

Two balls and two strikes.

Eli grinned as the crowd whooped and cheered. He repositioned on the mound.

Perfect game.

Well, not really. Two guys had hit off of him in the fifth inning and three had hit off of him, including a triple, in the sixth. The Friars were up by two but they hadn't scored in two innings and the infield was struggling.

But none of that mattered to Eli. He'd never been happier.

He was in the major freaking leagues. The air in the San Diego Friars ballpark seemed sweeter and more electric than any he'd breathed before. The grass seemed greener. The sky bluer. The leather of the gloves seemed softer, the stitches on the balls tighter and the lights on the scoreboard brighter.

There was a *feel* here that he soaked in every time, like the warm tingly sports cream the trainer rubbed into his shoulder muscles after each game.

Even the sports cream felt better here.

It wasn't his first game with the Friars. He'd been in California for three months now. It wasn't his best performance. He'd pitched four innings a month ago, giving up only two walks and two hits. It wasn't even the biggest game of the season. They were playing the Atlanta Braves, certainly not a big rival.

But it was his favorite game of the season.

Caitlyn was in her usual spot with the other team wives and girlfriends, just to the first base side of home plate. She sat next to Sadie Merritt, Caleb Hart's fiancée. They'd clicked right away, which worked out well since Caleb Hart had become Eli's mentor on the team. Between Caleb and Mike Solo, Eli had all the friends he needed in San Diego—or would, as soon as the Friars called up Trevor Stark. According to the rumor mill, any minute now the bad-boy slugger would be taking San Diego by storm. Eli couldn't wait. With Trevor in the lineup, there'd be no stopping the Friars.

Best of all, he had Caitlyn. She wore a snug white t-shirt advertising Scoop, the shop she was still working with back in Kilby. She looked gorgeous, as always, her smile bright, her eyes on him the entire time, her little hand signals—that they'd come up with one night while tangled in the bed sheets, talking and laughing—making him smile. Like when she put her sunglasses on top of her head. That meant he needed to stride out farther. When she tucked her hair behind her left ear it meant that he needed to throw harder. When she put her sunglasses back on her nose it meant he could relax, that he was doing well. And when she applied lip gloss that meant he was going to get a blow job later that night.

She had very soft lips from all of the lip gloss she used.

He'd bought her a ten-pack the other day at the store and left it on the pillow next to her when he'd gotten up to come to the park early today.

But none of that was unusual. It made his games, hell, his *life*, better having her there and being connected to her during the games that way. But it wasn't what had his level of excitement turned up to max.

What really had his nerves jumping today, in a good way, was that the box also held his father and sister, Caitlyn's mother, father and brother, along with a rowdy bunch from Sapphire Falls. Ty and Hailey were there, Peyton and her half-sister, Hope, with her husband TJ—who happened to be Ty's older brother as well—had come along; Peyton and Hope's dad, Dan, Levi and his wife

Kate, and Levi's brother Joe and his wife Phoebe.

And they were making their presence known. They had signs, special chants just for him, and were, in general, being loud and crazy.

Eli couldn't get enough of it.

This felt good. Right. Like he was exactly where he was supposed to be.

And while he always loved being on the mound, he was eager to get through the game and take them all out for a celebratory dinner.

He ran his fingers over the ball in his glove. He glanced at Caitlyn and saw her cross her arms.

That meant he needed to focus on what he was doing.

He grinned. Yeah. He supposed he needed to close out the game, with a win, before they could have that celebratory dinner.

He tugged on his earlobe. That meant, "yeah, yeah."

Then he looked to Mike Solo behind home plate.

And got the sign for a fastball.

Eli shook that off.

He could practically see Mike's eyebrow rise behind his mask. Eli almost never shook him off. Even though Mike was barely past the rookie stage himself, he already had league-wide reputation for brilliant pitch selection.

But Mike did give him a new sign.

The one he wanted.

Eli gave him a nod, pulled back, and went into his windup and delivered the pitch.

"Strike three!"

Exactly.

Knuckleball for the win.

He looked up at Caitlyn as his teammates whooped and jogged toward the infield for the traditional high-fives and fist bumps.

She grinned.

And slowly applied a new coat of lip gloss.

Yep, he was exactly where he was supposed to be.

ABOUT THE AUTHORS

Jennifer Bernard is a USA Today bestselling author of contemporary romance. Her books have been called "an irresistible reading experience" full of "quick wit and sizzling love scenes." A graduate of Harvard and former news promo producer, she left big city life in Los Angeles for true love in Alaska, where she now lives with her husband and stepdaughters. She still hasn't adjusted to the cold, so most often she can be found huddling with her laptop and a cup of tea. No stranger to book success, she also writes erotic novellas under a naughty secret name that she's happy to share with the curious.

You can find Jennifer on the web at JenniferBernard.net
On Facebook at
http://Facebook.com/JenniferBernardBooks
On Twitter at https://Twitter.com/Jen_Bernard
On Instagram at
https://instagram.com/jenniferbernardbooks/

Erin Nicholas is the New York Times and USA Today bestselling author of over thirty sexy contemporary romances. Her stories have been described as toe-curling, enchanting, steamy and fun. She loves to write about reluctant heroes, flawed heroines, sex with food and happily ever afters. She does not like to write dark moments, synopses or bios.

You can find Erin on the web at www.ErinNicholas.com
On Facebook at
https://www.facebook.com/ErinNicholasBooks
On Twitter at http://twitter.com/ErinNicholas
On Instagram at https://instagram.com/erinnicholasbooks/

Look for these titles by Jennifer Bernard

Now Available at all book retailers!

Love Between the Bases
All of Me
Caught By You
Drive You Wild (available June 28)

The Bachelor Firemen of San Gabriel
The Fireman Who Loved Me
Hot for Fireman
Sex and the Single Fireman
How to Tame a Wild Fireman
Four Weddings and a Fireman
The Night Belongs to Fireman

novellas
One Fine Fireman
Desperately Seeking Fireman
It's a Wonderful Fireman

Look for these titles by Erin Nicholas

Now Available at all book retailers!

Sapphire Falls
Getting Out of Hand (book 1)
Getting Worked Up (book 2)
Getting Dirty (book 3)
Getting In the Spirit, Christmas novella
Getting In the Mood, Valentine's Day novella
Getting It All (book 4)
Getting Lucky (book 5)
Getting Over It (book 6)
Getting to Her (book 6 companion novella)
Getting to the Church On Time, Wedding novella

The Bradfords
Just Right (book 1)
Just Like That (book 2)
Just My Type (book 3)
Just the Way I Like It (short story, 3.5)
Just for Fun (book 4)
Just a Kiss (book 5)
Just What I Need: The Epilogue (novella, book 6)

Anything & Everything
Anything You Want
Everything You've Got

Counting On Love
Just Count on Me (prequel)
She's the One
It Takes Two
Best of Three
Going for Four
Up by Five

The Billionaire Bargains
No Matter What
What Matters Most
All That Matters

Single titles
Hotblooded

Promise Harbor Wedding
Hitched
(book 4 in the series)

Boys of Fall
Out of Bounds
Illegal Motion

Enjoy this Excerpt from

Drive You Wild

Love Between the Bases

Coming June 28, 2106

by Jennifer Bernard

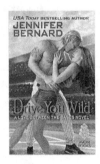

Footfalls raced after him. *Paige.* It had to be. Blood boiling, Trevor stopped at the head of the stairs and intercepted her, snagging her wrist and pulling her down the steps after him.

"What are you doing?"

"Rescuing you," he growled.

"From what? I'm perfectly fine."

"I haven't decided yet."

"What…that makes no…sense…" She continued to squawk as he hauled her down the stairs into the clubhouse. He knew it would be completely empty during the National Anthem. Even the clubhouse attendant would be out on the field.

Once inside the deserted, towel-strewn locker room, he spun her against the wall and braced his hands on either side of her head. "This," he ground out, "is a bad idea."

She stared at him with a bewildered expression. He

216

seized the opportunity to gaze his fill of her in the daylight, up close. Close enough to notice the outer rim of purple surrounding the sparkling blue of her eyes and the light spray of freckles across her cheekbones. A long strand of honey-brown hair clung to her neck. Fresh and alive, her apple fragrance lured him closer; he sensed the racing of her heart.

He eased off, in case it was fear causing her heart to beat so fast. "Why didn't you tell me who you were?"

A crease appeared between her eyebrows. He clenched his hands to keep from smoothing it away. "I told you my name."

"*Part* of your name."

"We didn't exactly meet at a formal tea party," she said. "I don't remember how I introduced myself."

"I do. Paige, you said."

"Well, it's Paige Mattingly Austin Taylor, since you seem to require the whole thing."

"The only part I'm worried about is the 'Taylor.' Your father despises me."

She held his gaze. "A legend like Crush Taylor doesn't like seeing talented players waste their gifts."

As if she'd suddenly caught fire, he released her. He wasn't wasting his gift, he was using it to protect his sister the best way he could. He paced away from her, rubbing one hand across the back of his neck.

"So last night you were in the parking lot waiting for Crush?"

"Yes. But I must have missed him, and then I saw you. And the man with the BB gun."

"Does Crush know that was you on the security tape?"

Her eyes widened in alarm. "No. And please don't tell him. He'd kill me. Or you. Maybe both."

"I won't tell him as long as you promise not to put yourself in danger like that again."

She pushed away from the wall and sauntered toward

him. "Um, I'm alone in an empty clubhouse with Big Bad Trevor Stark." On that word, she tilted her head back and swept past him. "Apparently danger is my middle name."

He followed her as she advanced farther into the clubhouse and peered curiously into the lockers. "I've never been in here before. It was always off-limits," she told him.

"Is that why you turned me down? No sleeping with the players?"

Outside Ramirez's locker, she turned to face him, folding her arms over her chest. With a mighty effort, he fought to keep his gaze away from the pretty curves of her breasts under her T-shirt. "I turned you down because our acquaintance consisted of about ten minutes of conversation while fleeing a man with a BB gun. Also because I was headed to see my father. Not only that, I'm not in the habit of sleeping with men I've only met once. I can probably come up with a few more good reasons. Is it really so strange?"

"In my life, it's unusual," he said simply. What the hell, it was the truth. Girls came on to him all the time.

A distant thumping sound told him the pregame ceremony had finished and the Catfish were taking the field. Normally, he'd be pissed as hell that he wasn't out there with them. Not this time. Talking to Paige in the empty quiet of the clubhouse, he didn't miss the baseball field. Strange.

Paige had scrunched up her face at his mention of his love life. "I think we can both agree that it's a good thing I turned you down, given who my father is. I hope your feelings aren't still wounded."

He shot her a sharp glance. "You know, suddenly I see the Taylor family resemblance. Crush always irritates the hell out of me too."

She bit her lip, amusement filling those big blue eyes. "I picked up on that."

218

"My *feelings* don't get wounded, so you can just put that worry out of your mind."

"Just like that, huh?" She flicked her fingers in the air. "What are you, some kind of emotionless robot?"

"Not at all. I have emotions. I get horny."

He used crudeness deliberately to get a rise out of her. But it only made one corner of her wide mouth lift, as if he'd issued a challenge. "Could have fooled me. We've been alone all this time and you haven't once made a move."

Narrowing his eyes, he closed the space between them. "Your taunts won't work. You rejected me, remember? That ship has sailed."

"Really? Where's the ship going?" She stepped forward. *Olimpia Milano,* that's what her shirt said, and damn him for not being able to keep his eyes off her. Those curves made the palms of his hands twitch, so he closed them into fists.

"Nowhere," he said firmly. This girl was trouble with a capital T—for Taylor.

"Are you afraid of the mighty Crush Taylor?" She took another step closer. "He's not as bad as he seems, you know."

"I'm not afraid of him." He placed his hands on her shoulders to keep her from coming any closer. Her warmth carried into his skin, into his being, as if it was igniting him from within.

"And I'm not afraid of *you*." She ducked underneath his hands in a quick move right out of the NBA. He took a step back and his calves hit the bench situated next to the lockers. She reached out in apology and suddenly they were right smack against each other, chest-to-chest.

Fire flashed down his spine, hot and urgent. He hauled her against him—oh, sweet Jesus, she felt good. Soft and firm and shapely and alive and fresh and…then her mouth was under his, her lips parting, her breath warm against his

219

mouth, her flesh lush and sweet. It wasn't a kiss so much as a head rush.

Her breasts pressed against him, soft and enticing. He growled and walked her backward, pinned her against a locker. Lifted her legs to wrap around his waist. His lack of pants meant the bare skin of her legs slid against his, a smooth friction that sent more blood to his groin.

She trembled in his arms and grabbed the back of his jersey. "Touch me," she whispered wildly. "Just touch me."

Her urgency threw fuel on the fire driving him. He adjusted her on his thighs and slid his hands under the edge of her shorts, her skin like warm silk against his palms. She pushed against him, grinding against his seeking fingers. *Wild. Fierce.* He reached for her heat, for wetness, for glory. And froze.

Crush Taylor's daughter.

He pulled his hand out of her shorts and released her so she slid to the floor. She would have stumbled if he hadn't held her steady. Eyes huge, mouth moist from his kiss, she stared up at him.

"I shouldn't have done that. I'm sorry." Closing his eyes against the temptation of her, he swiped his arm across his forehead. His face was damp with sweat. How had a simple kiss gotten him to this state?

"No, it was my fault," she whispered. "I wanted you to. Oh God. I'm sorry. I guess it's… I'm so embarrassed." She covered her face with both hands. Her ponytail fell forward and he pushed it gently behind her shoulder.

"Embarrassed?"

"I've been going through a divorce, and it's been awful, and sex became this *loaded* thing, it was never just fun or pleasurable. I guess I forgot what it felt like when… I shouldn't have gotten carried away like that, and just so you know, I tend to babble during awkward situations. Can we mutually block this out? Make a pact of denial?"

"Pact of denial," he repeated dumbly. He was still stuck

on the divorce part. She looked much too young to be married.

"Yes. This never happened." Her eyes clung to his, color flooding her face.

That didn't sit well with him. He wasn't about to forget something like this. Even now his hands pulsed with the memory of her touch. But if that's how she wanted it…

"Do we have to shake on it? Because I'm not sure I can touch you without wanting to throw you down and—" He broke off as her eyes went the starry violet of a Texas twilight.

"That's okay, we can make it a verbal agreement," she said in a slightly choked voice.

He looked down at the front of his jersey. "I'll have to have a talk with my nonverbal side, straighten a few things out."

She let out a bubble of laughter. "I'll leave that in your hands," she said, then turned scarlet. "I mean…
I'd…uh…better get to the owner's box before my father comes looking. Pact of denial?"

"Can we add in a pact of stay the hell away from each other?"

"That might be hard. I'm going to be working here. Mission 'Win the Championship' is now my life."

Just his luck, to share the hottest kiss of his life with a woman he couldn't go near. He ran his hand across the back of his neck. "You'd better go. There's a cold shower calling my name."

She hurried toward the exit. Damn those long legs. How would he ever forget the way they'd felt wrapped around his waist? "One question," he called after her. "Going through a divorce. Does that mean…?"

"It means I'm divorced." Her face was the bright red of a St. Louis Cardinals cap. "I'll see you around, Trevor Stark."

"See you, Paige Mattingly Austin Taylor."

With a fleeting smile, she whisked herself out of the clubhouse.

Pre-order today!

Getting His Way
Sapphire Falls

by Erin Nicholas

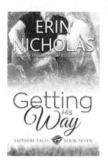

Coming May 10, 2016

Tessa Sheridan was sweet. Super sweet. Possibly the sweetest girl in Sapphire Falls. She was so sweet, she made her *own* teeth ache.

Which meant everyone was going to be very surprised when she stormed into the Come Again and chewed Bryan Murray's ass.

She pushed the door to Sapphire Fall's only bar open and stomped inside.

But her entrance was barely noticed. The music was loud and the place was full, especially around the bar where she had expected to find Bryan, the owner and main bartender on Thursdays, Fridays and Saturdays.

He was there behind the bar all right, but he was blocked from seeing the door by three gorgeous women and four of his adoring fans. The women didn't bother Tess. Two were married and the single one was interested in the town cop—even if she wouldn't admit it. The fans were guys who thought Bryan was the coolest, funniest, most inspirational guy they knew.

And the thing was, he was definitely cool, funny and inspirational.

In fact, Tess was about to yell at the guy who had inspired *her* and made her try something that had changed her life.

But she wasn't going to tell him that. Because Bryan Murray already had a hard time fitting his big head through doorways.

She took a deep breath and marched to the bar. She squeezed in between Ty and Tucker Bennett. Being squeezed in between those two was no hardship, but she kept her mad face fully in place as she leaned onto the bar and pointed at Bryan.

"I need to talk to you."

"Tess."

Bryan's face actually lit up when he saw her, and for just a second, she felt her heart flip and her frown ease.

No. She couldn't do that. She couldn't go all mushy over that smile—the way she had for the last twenty-five years.

"Can we talk?" she asked, keeping her voice firm and low.

Of course the people right around them—including Bryan's four adoring fans and the three gorgeous women with them— heard her.

And they all focused on her with rapt interest.

Bryan seemed to notice she wasn't overjoyed to see him and glanced around. "Actually, uh, I have a lot going on right now. Maybe later?"

She looked around too. The bar was busy, but everyone seemed happy with the level of their drinks. "Derek's here. I'm sure he can handle whatever comes up," she said. "It will only take a minute."

Maybe less. All she needed to tell him was to stay out

of her love life.

Could that wait until later? Maybe. Would it be better without an audience? Possibly. But she had come straight over after she'd heard he had warned off yet another guy from asking her out. She was ticked, and she needed to confront Bryan when she was ticked. And she needed to do it fast, before he wore her down and made her laugh and reminded her why she'd had a crush on him for as long as she'd known him.

Five years ago, if she'd heard that Bryan was keeping the other guys in town from dating her, it would had given her hope that he wanted something from her besides friendship. If he'd done it ten years ago, she would have assumed they were going to get married and live happily ever after. Of course, ten years ago—and fifteen years ago and twenty years ago and twenty-five years ago on the first day of kindergarten—a smile from him had meant they were destined to be together forever in her mind.

Now she knew better.

She had grown up. She had matured. She was thirty years old and had *finally* figured her life out. And she knew that Bryan thought of her as only a friend. Or maybe even a sister—though that thought made her shudder a little bit. Still, they'd known each other forever, and he had known that she was in love with him for most of her life. If he'd wanted more from her, he could have had it. Repeatedly. He hadn't even done anything to really encourage her romantic fantasies. Ever. She saw that now.

She had been young and naïve and starry-eyed over the guy since she was *five*.

Now she was none of those things.

She really needed to remember that.

"Not later," she said. "Now."

He was leaning against the counter on the backside of the bar and shifted to rest his elbows on the bar, putting his face directly in front of her. She moved back, not able to

225

handle having his face only inches from hers.

"Tess, let's do this after closing," he said, his voice almost soothing.

Soothing. Yeah. Then why did she feel like she'd just touched a live wire?

After closing, with no one else around, was *not* a good idea. If they were alone, she would revert to thirteen-year-old Tess…the girl with braces and oily hair and a big butt who would swoon every time he made a joke in math class. He could do no wrong in her eyes.

Back *then*. Definitely back then. Now she was smarter and more mature and knew that smiles and compliments didn't mean true love.

Tess lost her patience—something she never did. She slapped her hand down on the top of the bar, making the beer in Ty's and Tucker's mugs jump. "You're messing with me, Bryan, and it's got to stop."

He didn't look shocked. Or contrite. He cocked an eyebrow, looking almost impressed. Or something. "I'm messing with you?" he asked. He gave her a slow smile. "I really think I'd remember that."

That. That right there was the reason she couldn't be alone with him. Because he played the full-of-more-charm-than-sense-country-boy thing so well, and she fell for it every time. And because she knew there was more to him than that, and if she called him on the cocky-charm thing and he let the real Bryan show through, she'd be in even bigger trouble.

He didn't know that she knew there was more. He didn't know he had changed her life. He didn't know that she admired and respected him and that up until he had moved back to Sapphire Falls, she had planned to go to Denver to be near him.

And now he wouldn't know all of that. Because it didn't matter. She was going to Denver anyway. As soon as she had the money saved up.

"Very funny," Tess told him, narrowing her eyes. "You need to stop. You're starting to piss me off."

There was a beat of silence and then Bryan laughed out loud. And he wasn't the only one. Ty, Tucker, Kyle Ames, the town doctor, and Derek Wright, the main bartender all laughed too.

Tess crossed her arms and waited for them to sober up.

Finally, Bryan looked at her, still with a big grin. "That's cute, Tess."

Her eyes widened. Her being pissed off was *cute*?

So she didn't get pissed off much. She was a very forgiving, kind, *sweet* person. Overall. But she *could* get pissed. Probably.

Okay, pissed was pushing it. She was irritated, and confused, about Bryan's meddling with the guys who wanted to ask her out. But, yeah, probably not *pissed*.

Still, Bryan Murray needed to back off. He wasn't the guy she wanted anymore. Her life had changed three years ago when she'd read one of Bryan's blog posts for the first time and had started running. Her plans to ask him to coach her had made perfect sense then. So she'd started her move-to-Denver plan. Then *his* life had changed a year and a half ago. Now they just weren't on the same page.

She looked at Ty. "May I?" she asked, gesturing to his chair.

He grabbed his beer and stretched to his feet. "Please," he said with a grin.

Tess put a boot up on the rung of the bar stool and boosted herself up onto the seat. Then she got to her feet. The stool was made to swivel, and it did so slightly until Tucker grasped the back of it, steadying it for her. And *then* she realized she had a skirt on.

Well, crap.

She smoothed it down, pressed her knees together and straightened her back. Ty and Tucker wouldn't look up her skirt. Not with their wives, Hailey and Delaney, right there.

As for the others… She needed to get this over with.

"Excuse me," she said loudly.

But not loudly enough. Conversation, music and laughter continued around her.

Dammit.

She took a deep breath. *"Excuse me!"* she shouted.

That did the trick. Everyone in the room stopped talking and turned toward her. The jukebox continued to play Eric Church, but she didn't mind. Eric was one of her favorites.

"I just wanted to make a quick public service announcement," she told everyone.

She wasn't used to being the center of attention. She was the woman behind the people who were the center of attention. She had been Hailey's assistant for three years while the other woman had been mayor, and Tess now worked for the current mayor, TJ Bennett, Ty and Tucker's older brother. Her other jobs also put her behind the scenes most of the time. She taught yoga at Hope Bennett's studio, but being in front to lead a group through yoga poses wasn't the same thing as standing on a bar stool in the midst of the Come Again on a busy Friday night.

"It has come to my attention that some people have been misinformed about my dating habits," she said, feeling her chest and throat flushing pink. "I just wanted to clear up the fact that Bryan Murray is in no way in charge of my relationship status, and if anyone has questions about what I'm doing socially on any night of the week, you should contact me directly."

She breathed deeply and started to lean over to get down but realized just in time that if she bent over, her skirt would pull up in the back and would give Bryan an eye-full. She squatted instead, and grabbed the back of the stool. She felt a hand at her waist and she gave Tucker a grateful smile as he helped her down. Tess smoothed her skirt, licked her lips and headed for the door to the bar.

"Grab her."

Tessa heard Bryan's grim command, but she kept walking.

"I don't know if that's a great idea," Ty told him.

She kept walking.

"Dammit, Ty. *Someone* fucking grab her," Bryan said.

She turned back to tell him that he could go *grab* himself, but he was busy grabbing his forearm crutches and moving from behind the bar.

The starch went out of her spine instantly. He was coming after her, but he couldn't do it on his own because he had his hands full with his crutches. Crutches that he needed because of the biking accident he had been in eighteen months ago that had left him with a partial spinal cord injury. The reason he was back in Sapphire Falls. And the reason all of her plans had changed.

She felt like such an ass when she thought about all of that.

That damned accident. It had messed everything up. And, no, it wasn't all about her. Of course *Bryan's* life had been the one most impacted. But honestly, Bryan seemed less affected by it than the people around him were. Tess knew that his sister, Caitlyn, and his mother had had their lives turned upside down by it. She knew that Ty had changed his whole life after the accident—which he had been involved in as well, just not as badly hurt. She knew that all of the people in Denver who had trained with Ty and Bryan missed them both a lot. She knew Bryan's clients were feeling a huge loss.

But Bryan had continued to smile and laugh and inspire people through it all. He'd kept up with his blog—that she was certain he had no idea she even knew about, not to mention read on a regular basis—and he'd worked his ass off in rehab to the point where he could get around on crutches instead of a wheelchair most of the time and could go without anything occasionally.

He really seemed to be looking at the whole thing like

just another challenge to be met, and he was meeting it head-on.

But that challenge meant that Bryan was no longer a part of *Tessa's* plan.

That sounded horrible, of course, and she would never say it out loud to anyone. But since her plan involved running marathons, training in Denver and having a personal coach, Bryan was no longer on the list of possible candidates.

Since he had been the *only* candidate on her list until his accident, it kind of broke her heart.

Her runner's heart. Not her romantic heart. She had figured out a long time ago that Bryan wasn't a candidate for that.

Kyle was beside her a moment later, his hand on her upper arm. "Come on, Tess. Give him a chance," he said. "Don't make him hobble down the street after you."

See, that right there was part of this whole thing. Kyle mentioning Bryan hobbling was said so matter-of-factly because Bryan had encouraged that. He never shied away from talk of the accident or his resultant injuries and his permanent disabilities. He talked about them candidly and with humor and encouraged others to do the same. Everyone was very respectful, and no one felt uncomfortable around him. She admired that too.

How could she walk out on him now? She would look like a heartless bitch.

Even if she didn't care what others thought of her, she was not a heartless bitch.

She sighed. "Fine."

Bryan came up beside Kyle a moment later. "Does he need to carry you into my office?" he asked with a frown.

Bryan frowning was about as unusual as Tess standing up on a barstool and making a public announcement about her personal life.

"No," she said shortly.

"Then let's go." He turned and started for his office door.

Tess had no choice but to follow. And because she was behind him, and a red-blooded, heterosexual female who had loved him most of her life, she couldn't help but notice how wide his shoulders were and how hard his arms were and how not being able to run and bike like usual didn't seem to have taken one iota of tightness from his ass.

It was a partial spinal cord injury, so that meant he still had muscle activity in his lower body. From what she could see, it was an impressive amount. She knew he was doing a lot of swimming and working with what weights he could to improve and maintain his strength. He used the crutches, but he took fairly normal steps and moved quickly and with surprising grace. Using the crutches and wheelchair were no doubt a great workout for his upper body, but his butt and legs in the fitted, faded blue denim were certainly worth appreciating as well.

At the door, he stopped and turned the knob, then pushed it open and stood to the side, waiting for her to pass in front of him.

She did reluctantly.

She did *not* want to be alone with him. Even if there were fifty people on the other side of the door, being closed in his tiny six-by-six-foot office was a bad idea.

Because thirteen-year-old Tessa was never *that* far below the surface, and that Tess still loved Bryan Murray deeply.

Made in the USA
Las Vegas, NV
08 January 2023

65238826R00135